replica

Ice Cold

MARILYN KAYE

BANTAM BOOKS

NEW YORK · TORONTO · LONDON · SYDNEY · AUCKLAND

RL: 5.5, AGES 008–012
ICE COLD
A Bantam Skylark Book / February 2000

ISBN 0-553-48711-6

Visit us on the Web! www.randomhouse.com/kids
Educators and librarians, for a variety of teaching tools,
visit us at www.randomhouse.com/teachers

Published simultaneously in the United States and Canada.

Bantam Skylark is an imprint of Random House Children's Books, a division of Random House, Inc. SKYLARK BOOKS, BANTAM BOOKS, and the rooster colophon are registered trademarks of Random House, Inc. Bantam Books, 1540 Broadway, New York, New York 10036.

PRINTED IN THE UNITED STATES OF AMERICA

OPM   10   9   8   7   6   5   4   3   2   1

For Manée, Marie-Hélène, Vincent, Laurent L.,
Isabelle, Arnaud, Stéphanie, Bruna, Pierre, Carmen,
Marie, Laurent D., Nathalie, Stéphane D., Laura,
Jean François, Muriel, Jean Luc, Stéphane A., Louisa,
Thomas, Manuel, and Rosa—vous êtes formidables!

Ice Cold

one

Watching from her window, Amy Candler saw her best friend and neighbor, Tasha Morgan, coming out of the house next door. Amy flew downstairs and had her own front door open even before Tasha could ring or knock.

"Did you bring the magazines?"

Tasha patted the tote bag hanging from her shoulder. "Got them right here." She followed Amy into the kitchen and dumped the contents of the tote bag onto the breakfast table. Immediately Amy started poring over one of the fashion magazines.

"Ooh," she murmured. "Look at her." She indicated a photo, and Tasha looked but shook her head.

"Don't expect miracles, Amy," she said. "You'll never be able to make your hair curl like that."

"I know, I know," Amy said. "I'm just having some fantasies." She turned a few pages and admired another picture. "What about this one?"

Tasha made a face. "Oh, Amy, bangs are so last year."

Tasha's criticisms didn't sting at all. Amy was in a good mood that morning, and nothing could bother her. "I can't believe I'm actually getting my hair cut, finally!"

"What I can't believe is that you're letting your mother do the cutting," Tasha commented.

Amy shrugged. "It's not like I've got any choice. It's either Mom's Salon or my hair stays like this forever." She pulled off the towel that was wrapped like a turban around her head. Her wet, straight brown hair, freshly washed, fell limply below her shoulders.

"Your hair's not that bad," Tasha said. "But it does make you look about twelve years old."

"I *am* twelve years old," Amy pointed out. "And so are you."

"But you don't want to *look* it, do you?"

Amy couldn't argue with that. She continued to flip through pages. "What do you think of this style?"

Tasha looked. "Cute," she remarked. "And it says here that layers make you look more sophisticated."

Joining them in the kitchen, Nancy Candler was clearly alarmed at what she'd just heard. "Layers! I can't layer your hair, Amy, that's much too complicated. It's not like I graduated from beauty school."

"How *did* you learn how to cut hair, Ms. Candler?" Tasha asked.

"I watched a video," Nancy said. She glanced at the open fashion magazine on the table and bit her lower lip. "Oh dear . . . Amy, I can't do anything like that. How about a nice simple bob?"

"That's fine, Mom," Amy assured her. She could tell that her mother was nervous, and she didn't want her to chicken out. A simple bob might not be unique, but it was reasonably stylish and a whole lot better than the long hair she had now.

Tasha had an idea. "Could you angle it so the sides are longer, Ms. Candler? And maybe you could just make one or two layers—"

"Tasha!" Amy said. She could see the panic developing on her mother's face. "It's okay, Mom. I'll be perfectly happy with a bob."

She took a seat on top of the kitchen stool while Nancy arranged a hairbrush, comb, and scissors on the table. She covered Amy's shoulders with an old bedsheet and began combing Amy's wet hair. "Honey . . ."

"What?"

"Are you absolutely *sure* you want a haircut?"

"Absolutely," Amy said. "Mom, I have to start looking more mature."

"Why?"

Amy and Tasha exchanged looks. Parents never understood why it was important to appear older.

Tasha supplied an excuse. "Ms. Candler, you know that Amy was elected student council representative from her homeroom last week, don't you?"

"Yes, I do," Nancy said. "I'm very proud of her."

"Well, if she looks more mature, she'll get more respect from her classmates," Tasha declared.

Amy couldn't see her mother's expression, but she wondered if Nancy bought Tasha's rationale. Personally, she didn't think a haircut would make her classmates treat her any differently. "I still can't believe I won that election," she mused.

"And you beat Jeanine Bryant," Tasha added. "That has to feel good."

Amy didn't deny it. There was something very satisfying about winning an election where her opponent was the girl who had been her archrival since first grade. Then Amy flinched at the first sound of the scissors taking a cut out of her hair. To keep her mind off what was happening behind her back, she went on talking. "And I didn't even have to use any super-powers to win, either. All I did was make a speech in homeroom."

"What was the speech about?" her mother asked.

"Just how the student council should be more aware of what's going on at school, so the students can be more involved."

Tasha moved around behind Amy so she could better observe the transformation. "Are you sure that's even, Ms. Candler?"

Although she couldn't see her mother, Amy knew she was speaking through clenched teeth. "Tasha, please don't stand there, you're making me nervous."

"Sorry," Tasha said. She went to sit at the table across from Amy. "Did Jeanine make a speech too?"

"Not really," Amy said. She gasped a little as she felt another chunk of hair fall from her head. "She just said something like 'Vote for me,' and then she handed out big pink-and-white buttons with her name on them. The next day she gave out pens, and the day after, rulers. They were all monogrammed with her name."

"Wow," Tasha said. "She must have spent some serious money."

"I guess so," Amy agreed, trying very hard not to listen to the squeak of the scissors as they worked their way across her head. "But she's got plenty of money to spend. Did you see her new bag?"

Tasha nodded. "How could I miss it? She was dangling it in everyone's face. She made sure everyone saw the label so they'd know it wasn't one of those designer rip-offs. Did you see what she was showing off on Friday?"

Amy started to nod, but her mother said sharply, "Don't move," so she froze. But she certainly had noticed Jeanine's new acquisition. Lots of kids came to school with a Walkman, but she didn't know any other seventh-grader who had a portable CD player. "She says she buys at least five CDs every week."

"What kind of allowance does Jeanine get?" Tasha wondered.

"I don't know, but I'm sure she'll tell you if you ask her," Amy said. "Jeanine's never shy about showing off. Whatever she gets, it has to be more than *we're* getting." She raised her voice just slightly to make sure her mother caught that remark. Nancy didn't comment. Either she was concentrating on Amy's hair, or she just didn't want to get into another "Can I have a raise in my allowance?" discussion.

"It must be nice to be rich," Tasha sighed. "Ms. Candler, are Jeanine's parents millionaires?"

"The Bryants are wealthy," Nancy acknowledged.

"But I don't think Jeanine gets an outrageously huge allowance. Just last month, at a PTA meeting, Mrs. Bryant was asking other parents what they gave their kids every week. She said she didn't want to give Jeanine more than her classmates get."

Amy found that hard to believe. "Well, all I know is that I can't afford a portable CD player on *my* allowance."

"And all I know," her mother said, "is that you don't need a portable CD player."

"But think of all the money I'm saving you by not going to a professional hairstylist," Amy pressed. "Mom, what's taking so long? Are you cutting one hair at a time?"

"I'm doing the best I can," her mother said. "You don't want me to hack it all off, do you?"

"All this fuss over a normal haircut," Tasha mused.

"Yeah, well, it's not exactly normal hair," Amy reminded her.

Tasha studied her friend. "It's interesting, you know? I mean, your hair looks ordinary."

"Amy's hair *is* ordinary," Ms. Candler murmured as she made another cut. "But it holds information that could reveal something extraordinary."

"I know, I know," Tasha said. "Amy's DNA, her genetic information. All anyone has to do is stick one hair from Amy's head under a microscope and they'll know what kind of weird genes she has."

"Well, not just *anyone*," Amy corrected her. "The person would have to be a scientist, right, Mom?"

"Mmm," her mother responded. She was concentrating on Amy's hair.

"Then how come Amy can't go to a regular hair salon?" Tasha asked. "Most hairstylists aren't scientists."

"You know the answer to that, Tasha. There are people out there who want very much to identify Amy as . . . as a unique individual."

"You mean, as a clone," Amy said. Her mother always tried to avoid using that word. Amy used to dislike it too. At first it made her feel completely unnatural. But a clone was what she was, it was what she would always be, and it wasn't a dirty word. The more she used the word, the more comfortable she was with it.

"These people are very well organized," her mother continued. "They have contacts—recruits trained to identify genetically engineered humans—all over the place. A hairstylist, a postal worker, that boy who delivers our newspaper . . . anyone could be connected with the organization." She stopped cutting Amy's hair and looked at Tasha seriously. "You do understand that,

Tasha, don't you? You must never, never tell anyone what you know about Amy."

Amy could see that her best friend was a little offended that Ms. Candler would even suggest such a possibility. "She knows that, Mom," Amy said hastily. "And so does Eric." She grinned. "And for your information, Tasha, may I remind you that my genes are not weird, they're superior."

Tasha grinned back at her. "Yeah, like I could ever forget. You could wring my neck with one hand tied behind your back."

"I think you mean with one *finger*."

"Amy, keep your head still!" Ms. Candler commanded. "Don't joke, girls, this is serious business."

"No kidding," Tasha said. "Hair is a frame for the face. Changing a hairstyle can change a person's entire look."

"Tasha, I'm not talking about hair," Amy's mother said sharply. Then she sighed. "I'm sorry, Tasha, I don't mean to bark at you. I just don't want to hear either of you making jokes about Amy's condition. Once you stop taking it seriously, you might very well slip up and let someone else in on it." She snipped off some more hair and sighed. "Well, I guess I'm finished."

Amy looked at Tasha anxiously.

"It's okay," Tasha told her.

Amy hopped off the stool and ran into the foyer, where there was a mirror hanging on a wall. Looking at her reflection, she could see that her mother hadn't destroyed her hair. But she couldn't say she saw any great improvement either. It was the same straight brown hair, just shorter.

Standing behind her, Tasha spoke encouragingly. "It'll look better once it's dry. And you'd better hurry up. The party's at two."

The girls ran upstairs to Amy's room. "Have you ever been to Simone's house before?" Amy asked as she plugged her blow-dryer into a socket.

Tasha nodded. "Every year at exactly this same time. Simone's mother and my mother are on the same charity committee, so Mrs. Cusack always makes Simone invite me to her birthday parties. And my mother makes me go. I'm glad you were invited this year."

Amy switched on the dryer and aimed it at her head. "It's only because we were partners in a history project," she said, speaking loudly so Tasha could hear her over the noise. "I did almost all the work but I let her get half the credit. I guess this is my reward."

"It's a very cool house," Tasha told her. She spoke in a normal tone. Amy's supersensitive hearing meant that she could hear easily, even over the roar of the dryer. "They've got a massive patio and a huge pool, bigger than Jeanine's. And there's always amazing food. Oh, by the way, I'd better warn you. Jeanine and Linda will probably be at the party."

For once Amy thought she wouldn't mind encountering her enemy and her enemy's best friend. Because now that her hair was drying, she could see a real difference—and it was a very good difference.

Tasha could see it too. "Wow! You look great!"

With so much weight gone, Amy's shorter hair seemed to have a lot more life and body. It fell to just above her shoulders now, and it actually bounced. The new style made her face look rounder, less long and thin. She anticipated some real compliments at the party. Even Jeanine would have to notice, though it was unlikely *she'd* say anything nice.

Nancy was waiting anxiously at the bottom of the stairs. A huge smile of relief crossed her face when she saw Amy. "Well! Not bad, if I say so myself!"

Amy gave her mother a quick hug. "It's super, Mom, thanks! We'd better go, Mrs. Morgan's giving us a ride to the party. Can you pick us up?"

Nancy nodded. "Just call me when you want to leave. I'll be shopping with David, so you can call me on his cell phone."

"Is there something going on between your mom and Dr. Hopkins?" Tasha wanted to know as they ran next door.

"No, they're just friends," Amy said. She waved to the boy who was dribbling a basketball in the Morgans' driveway and wondered if her mother would ever feel about someone the way Amy felt about *him*.

With the ball in his hands, Eric came toward them. "Want to shoot some baskets?" he asked.

"No way," Tasha said.

"I wasn't talking to *you*," Eric said, but his kid sister wasn't offended. She ran into the house to get her mother.

"I can't either," Amy said. "We're going to Simone Cusack's birthday party." She struck a pose. "What do you think?"

Eric stared at her blankly. "About what?"

"About how I look!"

His expression remained blank. "You look fine. Like always."

"Eric! I just had five inches of hair cut off!"

"Oh! Right! I guess the sun was in my eyes. Gee, it's fantastic, you look really, really beautiful."

Amy sighed. "Eric, don't overdo it. It's okay, I'm not mad, you can't help being a guy."

Eric grinned. "Thanks for being so understanding. You sure you have to go to this party?"

Amy nodded. "I wish you could come too."

"To a seventh-grader's birthday party?" Eric asked in his haughtiest ninth-grade voice. "No, thank you. I wouldn't go even if I was invited." He followed Amy to the car, which his mother and Tasha were getting into. "Of course, I wouldn't mind eating a seventh-grader's birthday cake if somebody brought me a piece. Or two."

"Eric, you're such a pig," Tasha said in disgust. Amy laughed at Tasha's typical kid-sister response. As for Amy, she behaved like a typical girlfriend—she blew Eric a kiss and made a mental note to bring home as much birthday cake as she could carry.

two 2

Tasha was right about Simone Cusack's home. It had a big patio and a huge pool, which looked cool and inviting on this hot and muggy Sunday afternoon. The whole backyard was decorated for the party, with helium balloons floating overhead, colored lights, and paper streamers. About twenty seventh-graders, all girls, were gathered. Some had already changed into their bathing suits and were splashing in the water.

Amy and Tasha stopped to deposit their gifts on a table laden with colorfully wrapped packages. "What did you get her?" Tasha asked.

"Yellow butterfly clips," Amy replied. "What about you?"

"Hairpins with tiny satin roses attached."

Neither of them was a close friend of Simone's, but Simone was known for decorating her fluffy blond curls with lots of accessories. On this special occasion, her hair was covered with tiny, glittery bows.

As a hair-conscious person, Simone was the first to notice the change in Amy. "Amy, you look so cute!" she exclaimed. Two other girls immediately chimed in with more compliments, and Amy entered the crowd feeling very good about herself. When Layne Hunter said, "Amy, I *love* your hair," she knew she'd passed the fashion exam with flying colors. Layne was noted for being the most trendy, stylish girl in the seventh grade. Somehow she always managed to look at least two years older than everyone else.

"Thanks," Amy said.

"And congratulations on winning the student council election," Layne added. "I voted for you."

"Thanks again," Amy said.

Layne's voice dropped. "But you don't have to tell Jeanine that, okay?"

"I won't," Amy assured her. She understood the request. No one wanted to get on Jeanine's bad side. Not that Jeanine had any other kind of side.

Amy could see her ex-opponent at the other end of the patio, with Linda Riviera and a couple of other girls. Jeanine was demonstrating her new toy—a mobile phone—and her groupies were responding with appropriate sighs of envy. Layne followed Amy's glance.

"You guys aren't exactly tight, right?"

"Jeanine hardly speaks to me at all," Amy told her. Actually, that wasn't completely true. Jeanine never missed an opportunity to hit Amy with an insult or a snide remark.

But for a while at least, Amy managed to avoid putting herself within insult distance of Jeanine and enjoyed the party. She and Tasha changed into swimsuits and joined the others in the water. Spontaneous pool games were happening, and it was a lively scene. After almost an hour splashing around, Amy congratulated herself on having avoided Jeanine for so long. It hadn't been difficult, though—Jeanine wasn't in the pool. She and Linda were sipping sodas at one of the little patio tables.

"How come she's not in the water?" Amy wondered out loud to Tasha.

Tasha had heard the reason. "She's got her period. At least that's what she's been telling everyone."

It figured. Amy guessed that only about half of the seventh-grade female population had arrived at that level of puberty, so of course Jeanine would want everyone to know she was among the more mature group. Anyway, if Jeanine was staying on the patio, Amy was safe as long as she stayed in the pool.

But she couldn't stay there forever. Eventually the smell of burgers on the grill lured everyone else out of the pool and Amy had to get out too. She collected her hamburger, then moved on to the long picnic table, where salads and chips and other stuff were laid out. Jeanine was on the other side of the table, and Amy studiously avoided her eyes.

She helped herself to cole slaw and handed the serving spoon to Carrie, the girl next to her. "Thanks," Carrie said. "I really like your hair, Amy. When did you get it cut?"

"Just this morning," Amy said. "I'm not used to it yet."

Jeanine looked up. "You got your hair cut *today*?"

Amy stiffened. She knew something was coming. "Yes," she replied cautiously. "Why?"

"It's *Sunday*," Jeanine said. "Hair salons aren't open on Sunday mornings."

Amy considered this. She could lie and say that she'd found the one and only hair salon in Los Angeles that was open on Sunday mornings. But then Jeanine or someone else would want to know the name of the salon and where it was. There was no point in getting herself bogged down in a web of stories. So she confessed.

"My mother cut it."

She might as well have announced that her mother had removed her appendix. Jeanine let out a shriek of horror. "You let your *mother* cut your *hair*? What did you do, get bubble gum in it? Peanut butter?"

Amy spoke through clenched teeth. "No. I just felt like getting my hair cut."

Jeanine wouldn't let it go. "Why couldn't you wait until the real hair salons are open?" Then she clapped a hand over her mouth and spoke in a very loud whisper. "Oh, I'm sorry. Maybe you can't afford to go to a real hair salon."

Amy tried to think of a suitable comeback, but her superior skills didn't include that kind of quick thinking.

Layne spoke lightly. "Oh, who cares who cut Amy's hair? It looks good, that's what counts." Jeanine didn't acknowledge the remark but kept right on talking.

"Being poor is nothing to be ashamed of, Amy," she said, phony sweetness dripping from her lips. "You know, I have some old clothes that my mother was going to give to a charity. But you can have them."

By now all the girls at the table were silent, watching

and listening and waiting to see what Amy would do or say. Amy still couldn't come up with a suitable retort. Fortunately, Tasha could.

"Jealous much, Jeanine?"

Clearly Jeanine hadn't expected a remark like that. "Why would I be jealous?"

"Because Amy's on the student council and you're not."

Jeanine's face darkened for a second, but she recovered quickly. She turned to her pal Linda and spoke conversationally. "I think maybe you're right, I *should* demand a recount tomorrow. That vote was awfully close."

Amy allowed herself a brief smile. The vote hadn't been that close. Jeanine was simply determined to do anything she could to make trouble for Amy.

At least Jeanine's venom wasn't reserved for Amy. Jeanine didn't forget the way Layne had tried to smooth things over. They were all sitting around the patio, eating, when she took her revenge.

"Layne, how is your sister?" she asked. "I heard she was very sick."

"She's better," Layne said. "She was never all that sick."

"Really?" Jeanine asked. "I heard she was crazy and

your parents had to have her committed to a mental institution."

Layne flushed. "Excuse me, I need to use the bathroom." She got up and went inside the house.

"Is her sister really crazy?" someone asked.

It turned out that Layne's older sister had an eating disorder and was in a special treatment facility. Of course, Jeanine had made it sound like the girl was a raving lunatic, a psychotic serial killer or something.

Carrie mentioned Greg Dawson, an eighth-grade boy she had a crush on, and Jeanine had some gossip about him too. "Do you know why his parents got divorced? His father's gay, and he left his wife for his boyfriend. Can you believe it? Don't say anything to Greg about it, he's so embarrassed."

Tasha leaned over and whispered to Amy. "And so she tells a whole gang of people, so the word will get around and Greg will just be more embarrassed."

"What did you say, Tasha?" Jeanine asked.

"Nothing," Tasha said.

"I hope I didn't hurt your feelings. I mean, maybe someone in your family is gay." She pretended to gasp. "Oh, no! It's your brother, Eric, right?"

"Eric is not gay," Tasha shot back. "Not that there's anything wrong with being gay. But my brother isn't."

"I can testify to that," Amy chimed in.

"Really?" Jeanine asked. "Have you and Eric, you know, messed around a lot?" She uttered another artificial gasp. "Amy! Have you two gone all the way?"

That comment elicited a chorus of giggles, and Amy wanted to scream. Fortunately, at that very moment Simone's mother came out with a huge cake, and everyone started to sing "Happy Birthday." Simone blew out her candles, everyone applauded, and the cake was served, which kept Jeanine's mouth shut for a while. The next event was the opening of the gifts, and that held everyone's attention.

Simone received lots of hair accessories, some CDs, a cosmetics case, a biography of Leonardo DiCaprio, and a set of bubble bath powders in ten different scents. Everyone oohed and aahed over all the stuff. There were bigger gifts that had been sent by family members— a new backpack from her uncle, and a pretty silver bracelet with turquoise stones from a cousin.

Even Jeanine admired the haul. "Ooh, that's gorgeous," she crooned as Simone held the bracelet in the air for everyone to see. "I love turquoise!"

Having Jeanine's seal of approval clearly pleased Simone. She put the bracelet on right away. Once again Amy had to marvel at how much influence Jeanine had over her friends.

After the gifts, there was more food—all the ingredients for making milk shakes and sundaes. From the speakers on the patio music blasted, and some girls started dancing while others gathered around the ice cream table to check out the goodies.

That was when the accident occurred. Layne was showing everyone a swing dance step her mother had taught her, where one person took the other's hand and twirled them around. She grabbed Amy's hand to demonstrate, and as Amy twirled, she collided with Jeanine.

Amy's arm flew out. Her superior strength gave it more power than she intended it to have—and it hit Jeanine, propelling her forward, right into the deep end of the pool.

Commotion ensued. Jeanine screamed as if she was about to drown, which was ridiculous because she was an excellent swimmer. A couple of girls reached over and helped her out of the water. Then Simone and her mother escorted Jeanine into the house so she could get out of her wet clothes and borrow something of Simone's to wear. Amy called out apologies to Jeanine, but everyone assured her that the accident hadn't been her fault and nobody blamed her.

Amy had a pretty solid feeling that the victim wouldn't excuse her so easily. When a calmer, drier

Jeanine emerged from the house, Amy knew she had better prepare herself for retaliation. At least she was still wearing her bathing suit.

But Jeanine was more creative than Amy gave her credit for. Amy was totally unprepared when Jeanine took her revenge. As Amy sat by the gift table, flipping through the Leonardo DiCaprio book, she suddenly became aware of something wet and cold and thick sliding down the side of her head.

"Oh, I'm so sorry!" Jeanine cried out, but not before she'd managed to dump an entire strawberry milk shake on Amy.

Moments later, in the bathroom, Amy realized that there was no way she could get the sticky gunk out of her hair without a thorough washing. Simone stood helplessly by with a towel.

"I think I'd just better go home," Amy told her.

"Sorry about that," Simone said. "But you know how Jeanine is. Honestly, sometimes I think she's truly evil."

Amy was mildly surprised to hear Simone say that. "Then why did you invite her to your birthday party?"

Simone made it obvious that she considered this a silly question. "Amy, she's *only* the most popular girl at school."

"It's weird," Amy said. "Practically no one likes her, but everyone sucks up to her."

Simone shrugged. "That's just the way it is, I guess. But between us, sometimes I think she's the devil in disguise."

Strong words, Amy thought. But not a bad definition of Jeanine Bryant.

three

I t felt strange, walking alone to school the next morning. But student council always met before homeroom, and Amy didn't want to ask her best friend or her boyfriend to get up that early. They both liked their sleep too much, especially Eric.

So did Amy, but it wasn't so bad for her. Normally the walk to school took twenty minutes. But if she was careful to take side streets and move through alleys, where people wouldn't notice her, she could use her extraordinary speed and make the trip in five minutes. It was one of the benefits of having been engineered from superior genetic material. It also allowed her to stay in bed an extra fifteen minutes.

Parkside Middle School had a different feeling before the first morning bell. Teachers were there, and some students had arrived for practices or club meetings, but it was quiet compared to the commotion Amy was accustomed to. She felt special, walking through the nearly empty hallways.

Student council met in a classroom on the second floor. Amy knew there would be eighteen representatives, six from each grade, plus the president of the student body, Cliff Fields. She would be the only new rep, a replacement for a girl who had moved away.

Only about half the kids were already there. Amy took a seat at the back of the room, which was appropriate for a lowly seventh-grader and new member. Hoping to recognize someone, she looked around. Parkside was a big school, and Amy didn't even know all the kids in her own grade. So she was pleased to see Carrie, the girl from Simone's birthday party, on the other side of the room. They smiled and waved at each other.

Amy recognized Cliff Fields, the student body president, who held a gavel in his hand. He was talking to two adults. One was Ms. Carroll, the assistant principal, who was also advisor to the student council; the other was a gaunt, stern-faced woman who seemed vaguely familiar. Then, looking very important, Cliff went to the desk at the front of the room and rapped the gavel.

"I call this meeting of the Parkside Middle School student council to order."

Amy leaned forward attentively, eager to hear about all the exciting activities. But exciting wasn't the word for what came next.

"The secretary will read the minutes from the last meeting," Cliff said.

A girl rose from her seat and read from a notebook in a monotone. "The meeting was called to order by President Fields at eight oh one A.M. Secretary Donato read the minutes from the previous meeting. Josh Levin moved to approve the minutes. Michelle Unser seconded the motion. The minutes were approved unanimously.

"Vice President Keane called the roll. Representatives Kelly and Cohen were absent without excuse. Treasurer Polanski reported that there was forty-three dollars and twenty-six cents in the budget. President Fields called for announcements. Ms. Carroll announced that some students have been throwing paper trash into the plastic trash bin in the cafeteria.

"President Fields called for old business. There was no old business. President Fields called for new business.

There was no new business. The meeting was adjourned at eight oh six A.M."

The girl sat down.

"Is there a motion to approve the minutes?" Cliff asked.

"I move to approve the minutes," someone called out.

Cliff nodded. "Motion to second?"

Another representative said, "Yeah, move to second."

"All in favor?"

Hands went up.

"Opposed?"

No hands went up.

"The minutes are approved as read," Cliff said. "The vice president will take the roll."

For Amy, this was slightly more interesting than the minutes. She got to say "Here" when her last name was called, and she learned that Carrie's last name was Nolan.

The treasurer reported that the budget was exactly the same as it had been the week before. Then the president called for announcements.

Ms. Carroll rose. "I have two announcements. First, I would like to introduce Dr. Holland. Dr. Holland is the new head of our guidance department. Dr. Holland, would you like to say a few words to our school leaders?"

The other woman rose, her grim expression still intact. "I am a psychologist. My specialty is anxiety and depression in the young adolescent. Please remember that the guidance staff is here to help you with any personal problems you may have, as well as academic problems. Share your feelings with us." She punctuated this command with another stern glare, and then she sat down. Amy tried to imagine sharing any feelings with Dr. Holland. She decided she'd rather share them with a large rock.

Ms. Carroll continued. "My second announcement deals with a very disturbing situation. There have been a series of thefts here at Parkside. School supplies are disappearing in large quantities. Boxes of pencils, three cartons of paper, five staple guns, and a can of photocopy machine fluid have vanished. Last week an overhead projector was taken from the media room. Our custodian, Mr. Nevins, reports that three new classroom wastebaskets are missing. If anyone knows anything about this, you must come forward at once with your information."

Amy perked up at this bit of news. Why would anyone steal staple guns and wastebaskets? It sounded intriguing.

Cliff Fields thanked Ms. Carroll and Dr. Holland, and the two women left the room. Cliff then asked if there was any old business. Since there had been no new business the week before, Amy wasn't surprised when no one spoke up.

"Any new business?"

Amy looked around. No one had a hand up, so she raised hers. Cliff stared at her. "What do *you* want?"

Amy swallowed. "I—uh, I just want to bring up, um, some new business." A stillness fell over the room. It was as if she'd just proposed burning down the building.

Cliff was still staring at her. "What new business?"

"Well, Ms. Carroll was just telling us about all this stuff that's disappearing from school. Shouldn't we be talking about that? Maybe we could do something."

"Something like what?" Cliff asked.

"Well, we could ask questions, start investigating . . ." Amy's voice trailed off when Cliff gave her a patronizing smile.

"It looks like we've got a Nancy Drew wannabe on the student council," he cracked, and a couple of kids laughed. Amy flushed. Cliff then spoke in a tone that was so kind and fatherly she wanted to kick him. "Amy, if you see anyone walk out of school with a wastebasket, you can let us know. Any other new business? No?" He rapped his gavel on the desk. "All in favor of adjourning the meeting, say aye."

A chorus of voices said aye.

"Any nays?" Cliff asked.

No one responded. Amy hadn't said aye, but she didn't speak now either.

"Meeting adjourned," Cliff said.

Amy gazed around in dismay. Was this a typical student council meeting? If so, what was the big deal about being a member?

She waited at the door for Carrie and asked her, "Does the student council ever do anything?"

Carrie thought about it. "We have a canned-food drive at Thanksgiving," she said. "And we decorate a float for homecoming."

"Is that all? Why does everyone want to be on it?"

Carrie grinned. "So we can all go around saying we're on student council."

Amy sighed. This was turning out to be a major disappointment. "I still think we should try to find out who's stealing the stuff from school."

"Okay," Carrie said cheerfully. "If you have any ideas, let me know."

But Amy didn't have any ideas at all. "I suppose it could just be a prank," she said. "Someone trying to make trouble. Maybe it's those kids who wrote all that graffiti on the school doors last summer."

"Or maybe Jeanine Bryant's stealing the stuff and selling it to other schools," Carrie said.

Amy was startled. "What?"

"Just kidding," Carrie assured her. "But she's got to be getting money from somewhere. Look at her!"

Amy realized that Jeanine was in the group coming down the hall. She had her mobile phone to her ear, and she was talking loudly—probably so everyone would notice that she had a mobile phone. As usual, she was the center of attention, and the girls around her seemed to be admiring her fringed suede coat.

"You see that jacket?" Carrie asked. "It cost six hundred dollars. And her parents don't even know she has it. She keeps it in her locker here at school."

"Wow," Amy breathed. So her mother had been right. Jeanine's new wealth really wasn't coming from her parents. From where, then? This was even more interesting than the missing school supplies.

Amy parted from Carrie and went to her homeroom. Jeanine entered just in front of Amy. The classroom was warm, so Jeanine took off her jacket, but she carried it over her arm, carefully folded so that the label showed. Amy couldn't help wondering if Jeanine had gotten into shoplifting. She knew there were girls who made regular trips to department stores to pick up small items—lipsticks or hair clips. But how could anyone walk out of a store with a fringed suede jacket? It wasn't like you could hide it in a pocket.

Or in a handbag. She glanced over at Jeanine's leather bag, which lay on her desk. No, the bag was much too small for a jacket. Even so, as Jeanine opened it, Amy focused her superior vision. It would be interesting to see if there were lots of shiny new cosmetics inside, and she watched closely as Jeanine threw in her phone.

Amy didn't see any cosmetics. But as Jeanine took out a pencil, Amy did spot something shiny among the contents of the bag. A silver-and-turquoise bracelet. The bracelet she'd seen the day before at Simone's birthday party.

four

When they met at their usual table for lunch that afternoon, Amy told Tasha what she had seen in Jeanine's bag. "Remember how she went wild over Simone's bracelet at the party? The one that Simone's cousin sent? Well, Jeanine must have gone right out and bought herself one exactly like it."

Tasha looked thoughtful. "Are you sure about that?"

"I saw it," Amy insisted. "It's absolutely identical."

"No, that's not what I mean." Tasha was so deep in thought now that she actually ate a forkful of cafeteria mystery meat without wrinkling her nose. "Are you absolutely sure she *bought* the bracelet?"

Amy's eyes widened. "Tasha! You think she *stole* it?"

"Think about it," Tasha said. "I heard Simone tell someone that her cousin lives in Arizona, and that she bought the bracelet on an Indian reservation out there. As far as I know, there aren't any Indian reservations in Los Angeles."

Tasha was right, of course. That hadn't even occurred to Amy. "But I'm sure there are stores in L.A. that sell Native American jewelry," she pointed out. "She could have bought it here."

"When?" Tasha countered. "Yesterday was Sunday, and most stores were closed. She couldn't have bought it this morning—the stores wouldn't have been open yet."

Tasha's logic was unbeatable. Still, Amy was finding the idea of Jeanine as a thief hard to take. "But when did she steal it? At the party, in front of everyone?"

Tasha didn't have a chance to reply. Layne and Carrie appeared by their table. "Hi, can we join you?" Layne asked.

"Sure," Amy and Tasha chorused, and the two girls sat down. With a quick shake of her head, Amy communicated to Tasha that she didn't want to go on talking about Jeanine in front of the other girls. It was very possible that both Layne and Carrie disliked Jeanine as much as she and Tasha did, but Amy didn't feel right starting rumors about Jeanine's being a thief.

Layne and Carrie had both brought lunches from home, and when Carrie unwrapped a piece of Simone's birthday cake, the others looked at it longingly.

"I took a piece home too," Layne said, "but I ate it for breakfast. Did you guys bring any cake home?"

Amy nodded. "My boyfriend, Eric, ate it all."

"He's such a pig," Tasha put in. Hastily she added, "It's okay, I can say that because he's my brother."

"Simone got some great presents," Layne commented. "I liked the bracelet a lot."

Amy practically choked on a carrot stick. Carrie slapped her on the back. "Are you okay?"

"I'm fine," Amy managed to say.

"Your hair still looks good," Layne commented. "No one would ever know you'd had a milk shake dumped on your head yesterday."

"It was pretty gross," Amy admitted. "I had to wash my hair three times and use half a bottle of conditioner on it."

"That was a crummy thing for Jeanine to do," Carrie noted. "And I don't believe for one minute that it was an accident."

It wasn't easy, but Amy tried to be fair. "I guess she thought I pushed her into the pool on purpose."

"No way," Layne said. "She was just looking for an excuse to do something mean and nasty. It's just the way she is."

It comforted Amy to know that others shared her feelings about Jeanine. Jeanine was undoubtedly a mean and nasty girl.

But that didn't make her a thief. "I still can't believe she's stealing things," Amy told Tasha on the way home that afternoon.

Tasha shrugged. "It would explain why she suddenly has all that new stuff."

"Simone's in my history class," Amy said. "She didn't say anything about the bracelet being missing."

"She probably thinks she lost it at home," Tasha declared.

"Maybe she hasn't noticed that it's missing yet."

"What if we call her when we get home," Amy said, "and innocently ask her about it?" If the bracelet was missing, Amy suspected that Simone would confront Jeanine and tell her how she'd found out that Jeanine had it. And there was no telling how, when, or where Jeanine would get back at Amy. It was becoming pretty complicated—and ridiculous. With an entire organization of bad guys who wanted to find her and kidnap her and experiment on her, Amy knew she was silly to worry about one dumb classmate.

40

Happily, when they turned onto their street, there was a distraction. "Isn't that Dr. Hopkins's car?" Tasha asked.

Amy snapped her fingers. "Oh, right, it's Monday. You want to come in and say hi?"

Dr. David Hopkins had been coming by the Candler home on Monday afternoons ever since an awful fever had temporarily altered Amy's superior genetic structure. Amy thought she was pretty much back to normal now, but she didn't mind having Dr. Hopkins check her out. He was the only doctor who was allowed to get near her. Nancy Candler didn't trust medical people any more than she trusted hairdressers.

But Dr. Hopkins was an exception. He was an old friend of Nancy's, as well as a former colleague. They had worked together on Project Crescent, the top-secret government experiment that had resulted in the creation of twelve identical female clones. He knew all about Amy.

They found Dr. Hopkins sitting at the kitchen table with Amy's mother. He was speaking softly and intensely. Tasha sighed as she and Amy peeked into the kitchen from the living room. "Ooh, Amy, they look like they're getting romantic," she said in a low voice.

"Wishful thinking," Amy said. She had no problem seeing a relationship develop between her mother and

Dr. Hopkins, since it would distract her mother from constantly worrying about her. Plus, Dr. Hopkins was a good guy, and it was nice having him around.

But Amy could pick up bits of their conversation, and there was nothing romantic in their discussion of random molecular distribution, whatever that was.

"Hi, girls," Nancy said when they went into the kitchen. "How was school?"

"Fine," they both replied automatically. Tasha was looking at a plate of cookies on the table. "Are those pecan chocolate chip?" she asked hopefully. There were only two left.

"Yes, and I was just about to put in another batch," Nancy said. "Why don't you stay here and help me while David checks Amy?"

So Tasha remained in the kitchen while Amy and Dr. Hopkins went into the living room. "How have you been feeling?" he asked her.

"Great," she told him. "I think I'm just about back to normal. Well, normal for me."

"Give it time," he cautioned her. "You were very sick, you know." He went through a regular routine, looking in her ears and eyes, listening to her heart, taking her pulse. Amy watched his face carefully for a sign that would tell her how she was doing. She knew better than to ask—Dr. Hopkins liked total silence so he could concentrate. Besides, he would never commit himself to anything before he was completely sure.

Next he put her through some exercises to check her strength and reflexes, her vision, and her hearing. He used a variety of instruments and paused every few moments to make notes. He'd nod or frown, and sometimes he'd mumble to himself.

Amy couldn't take it any longer. "How am I? Am I back to where I was before the fever?"

"Let me do some calculations," he said.

He spread out his papers on the coffee table. While he studied his notes, Amy concentrated on hearing the conversation in the kitchen. Apparently Tasha had told Nancy the story of Simone's bracelet, because Nancy was saying, "You can't accuse someone of theft unless you have very good evidence." They appeared in the living room with more cookies and a pot of tea, and Amy was ready with a response to her mother's comment.

"I *saw* the bracelet in Jeanine's bag, Mom. Don't you think that's enough evidence?"

"But you don't know how it got there," her mother said. "Maybe Jeanine borrowed the bracelet to wear for a day."

Amy and Tasha looked at each other. "I never thought of that possibility," Amy admitted. "I guess Simone could have loaned it to her."

"Well, there's one way to find out," Tasha said. "Let's call Simone and ask her."

"Or we could call Jeanine," Amy suggested. "Then she can't accuse me of talking about her behind her back."

They went into the kitchen to use the phone, but just as they approached it, it rang. "Hi, Amy, it's Monica. Is your mother busy?"

"Mom!" Amy called. "It's Monica!" Nancy came into the kitchen and took the phone. Amy knew from experience that her mother and their next-door neighbor, Monica Jackson, could stay on the phone for ages.

"If we don't call Jeanine right now, we're going to chicken out," Tasha warned her as they headed back into the living room. She had an idea.

"Dr. Hopkins, could we use your cell phone?"

"Mmm." The doctor nodded toward the coatrack in the foyer, where his jacket was hanging. Amy could see the mobile phone poking out of a pocket. She retrieved it while Tasha looked through the school directory for Jeanine's phone number.

"Of course, Jeanine has her own private line," Tasha noted.

Amy examined the phone. "Remember the last time I had to use one of these? I couldn't make it work. Do you know how?"

Tasha had never used a mobile phone before either, but it didn't seem all that difficult. She tried a couple of buttons until she got a dial tone; then she punched in Jeanine's number and gave the phone back to Amy.

"Hello, this is Jeanine. I'm not home right now, but you can call me on my mobile phone"—Jeanine gave the number—"or you can leave a message here after the beep."

"How many phones does one person need?" Amy muttered. She punched a button, thinking it would disconnect her. It didn't. She pressed another one and finally got a dial tone again. Then she dialed Jeanine's mobile number.

"Hi! I'm busy right now so I can't take your call. You can leave a message after the beep." Tasha could hear Jeanine's recording too, and she made a face. "What's she so busy doing? Looking in a mirror?"

"Shhh," Amy hissed. "She'll hear you." Then she realized Jeanine would be able to hear *her* voice too. Well, there was nothing she could do about that now.

"Hello, Jeanine, this is Amy. There's something I wanted to ask you. Please call me." Amy recited her phone number.

Her mother returned to the living room just as Dr. Hopkins put down his notes and looked up with a smile. "Amy, you're looking good. Almost back to normal. Your eyes and ears are operating at ninety-five percent compared to where they were before the fever. We can assume that your body and your brain are at the same level."

"Which still means stronger and smarter and better than everyone else," Tasha said, pretending to pout.

"Hey, that's not my fault," Amy said. "I didn't ask to be cloned in a laboratory."

"Ms. Candler, how many people were used to make Amy?" Tasha asked.

Nancy looked at Dr. Hopkins. "Do you remember, David?"

" 'Genetic material was gathered from eighty-four sources,' " he recited from memory. " 'They were carefully selected for their special skills and talents and strength and intellect.' "

"And all twelve Amys got exactly the same genes?" Tasha asked.

"Exactly," the doctor said. "But that doesn't mean they'd all be identical today. In appearance, yes, but the way a person is raised can have a lot to do with her development."

Nancy nodded. "Well, no one in this house is going

to develop unless I get some dinner started. Tasha, are you staying for dinner?"

"It's macaroni and cheese," Amy told her.

"I'll call my mother," Tasha said. She picked up the mobile phone and hit a button. "Funny, there's no dial tone. I think I pressed the same button as before."

Dr. Hopkins took it and listened. "Umm, I don't know what you did." He hit a button himself. "There, I hear a dial tone now." He handed the phone to Tasha and looked at Nancy. "Macaroni and cheese, huh?"

Nancy smiled. "Yes, David, you're invited too." Then she frowned at Tasha and Amy. "What are you two giggling about?"

"Nothing," they chorused, but as soon as Nancy's back was turned they gave each other a thumbs-up sign.

f5ve

Jeanine didn't get back to Amy that evening, and Amy really wasn't surprised. After all, she and Jeanine were definitely not in the habit of talking on the phone. And obviously curiosity hadn't propelled Jeanine to return the call.

"You can talk to her in homeroom," Tasha urged the next morning as they hung out in the hall before the bell.

But Amy wasn't comfortable with that. "There are too many kids around. She'll just throw a fit and call me a liar. Then she'll start crying so everyone will feel sorry for her and they'll be mad at me."

"Pass her a note," Tasha suggested. "Tell her it's important and ask her to meet you in private."

Amy liked that idea. Their homeroom teacher was pretty strict, and note-passing was reserved for communicating serious information. It was considered highly dishonorable for anyone to read a note while passing it to the person it was addressed to. Jeanine wouldn't be able to ignore a message sent that way.

But once she was settled in her homeroom seat, Amy began to wonder if passing a note was such a good idea after all. Jeanine didn't look like she'd be particularly receptive to any sort of communication from Amy. Normally, if their eyes met in class, Jeanine would act like Amy didn't exist. But this time, she actually seemed to be watching Amy. Every time Amy glanced in her direction, Jeanine was staring at her.

It was weird, and Amy wished her powers extended to mind reading. Sometimes she almost thought she could read minds, because she was so good at interpreting people's expressions. She was sensitive to feelings, and she could almost always tell when someone was angry or hurt or nervous. But not this time. Jeanine's expression was totally unreadable. It was almost like she was *studying* Amy. And it gave Amy the creeps.

The creepy feelings lasted all through homeroom,

and Amy no longer wanted to have any encounter with Jeanine at all. The second the bell rang, she shot out of the classroom and made her way directly to her next class. That was when she saw Simone in the hall.

"Simone!"

The girl looked up and paused. "Hi, Amy."

Now that she had Simone's attention, Amy tried to think of a reason for stopping her. "Um, I just wanted to thank you again. That was a neat birthday party. It was even worth getting a milk shake dumped on my head!"

Simone smiled, but there was no warmth or humor in her expression. "Thanks," she said, and turned away. Amy turned with her and stayed by her side as she walked down the hall.

"You got some cool presents," she continued. "Like that bracelet from your cousin." She looked pointedly at Simone's wrists and pretended to be surprised. "How come you're not wearing it?"

Simone didn't answer. Maybe she couldn't hear Amy in the hubbub of all the students changing classes. Amy repeated the question. "Why aren't you wearing your new bracelet?"

Simone spoke with clear reluctance. "I don't have it anymore."

"Did you lose it?"

"No. It's just that—well, I really didn't like it all that much. So I gave it away."

"Really? Who to?"

"Jeanine." Simone looked very relieved to find they'd reached her classroom. "See you later," she said, and darted inside.

Amy remained in the hall and went over this new information. So Simone had willingly handed over the bracelet to Jeanine. She supposed it really wasn't any of her business if Simone wanted to give it away. But an instant replay of her memory said something else. She recalled Simone's expression when she opened the gift at the party. She had definitely *liked* that bracelet.

Of course, Simone could have been faking it. Most people pretended to be pleased with a gift they didn't like in order not to hurt the giver's feelings. But Simone's cousin hadn't been at the party.

Amy peered into the classroom where Simone had taken a seat. She wasn't talking to anyone, and her face told Amy that something was bothering her. Concentrating on Simone's eyes, she caught the glimmer of tears forming.

A boy pushed past Amy to get into the room, and she spoke up impulsively. "What class is this?" she asked him.

"Study hall," he mumbled as he went in.

She remembered the previous month, when she and Simone had been working on that history project together. They'd complained about the fact that their study halls were in different periods and they couldn't work in the library together until after school. Right now Amy had language arts, and if she didn't run down the hall pronto, she was going to be tardy.

But she had a feeling this would be worth a demerit. As the bell rang, she strode into Simone's classroom and went directly to the man sitting at the front desk.

"Excuse me, Simone Cusack and I are working on a project together. Can she get a pass to go to the library with me?"

Thank goodness the teacher didn't ask to see *her* pass. He called Simone to his desk. Simone approached warily, looking back and forth between the teacher and Amy. The teacher took a pass from the stack on his desk, scrawled *library* on it, and handed it to Simone. Simone stared at it blankly.

"Come on," Amy said to her. "We've got work to do." Looking confused, Simone followed her out of the room.

The hall was deserted. Simone looked at the pass in her hand. "Amy, what's this for? We finished our project."

Amy didn't waste any time. "I want to talk to you about your bracelet."

She didn't need any unusual sensitivity to realize that Simone's whole body had stiffened and that the confusion on her face had turned into nervousness. "I *told* you. I didn't want it, Jeanine loved it, so I gave it to her. It's no big deal."

"I don't believe you," Amy said bluntly.

At that moment they were approached by a hall monitor, who demanded to see a pass. Amy took Simone's and showed it to him.

"You're supposed to be in the library," he said.

"That's where we're going," Amy assured him. In silence the two girls moved quickly to the end of the hall, up the stairs, and around a corner to the library's media center.

Amy was relieved to see that the nice librarian was on duty, the one who let you talk if you kept your voice down. She and Simone went to the most private table in the room, which happened to be sandwiched between two high shelves of reference books.

Simone was looking pretty tense as they sat down. Amy could tell she didn't want to be there. But she wasn't walking away, either, and that was a sign that maybe she really wanted to talk. Amy didn't beat around the bush.

"You didn't *give* that bracelet to Jeanine, did you? And you didn't sell it to her, or lend it to her either."

Simone said nothing, but she didn't deny it.

"Jeanine *made* you give her the bracelet, didn't she?"

"No," Simone said vaguely, but her eyes said the opposite.

"How did she get it from you? Did she promise you something?" And then Amy thought of a more likely reason why Jeanine would have Simone's bracelet. "Did she *threaten* you?"

"No," Simone whispered, but this time her eyes filled with tears, and Amy knew she'd hit on the answer. She groaned.

"That's so Jeanine. What did she say to you? 'Give me your bracelet or I'll make you unpopular'? She's not *that* powerful, Simone. Everyone knows she hates me, and I'm not unpopular."

But the tears that had formed in Simone's eyes were now rolling down her cheeks. And Amy knew there had to be something more going on here. "Simone? How did she threaten you?"

The words came out haltingly. "She said—she said she'd tell everyone about . . ." Her voice broke off.

Amy tried not to sound impatient. "About what? Look, if she's making up some story about you, don't worry. Tasha and I will tell everyone it's a lie."

Simone shook her head violently. "No, you don't understand." She looked around furtively, and her voice dropped to a level even Amy had difficulty hearing. "She said she'd tell everyone about my dad."

Amy didn't remember seeing anyone who looked like a father at Simone's party. That wasn't unusual. Lots of kids didn't have a father around the house. "What about your father?" Amy asked. Then she could see that Simone was supremely embarrassed. "Look, you don't have to tell me if you don't want to. But if you want to talk about it, I promise not to tell a soul."

The tears were gone, but Simone's eyes were still shining. "Promise?"

"Absolutely."

"He's in jail," Simone whispered.

"Oh."

"He didn't kill anyone or anything like that," Simone added hastily. "He used to work in a bank, and he . . . he took some money. I don't know how Jeanine found out. But she did."

"Oh," Amy said again. She didn't know what else to say about Simone's father. But she knew what she wanted to say about Jeanine. "So Jeanine said if you didn't give her your bracelet, she'd tell everyone that your father is in jail."

Simone nodded miserably.

"You know what that's called, Simone? Blackmail!" Even as Amy said the word, she was having a hard time believing it. This wasn't a TV cop show, this was middle school! "And you know what that makes her?" she continued. "A criminal!"

"But so's my father," Simone said. "And I don't want anyone to know that. You *promise* you won't tell anyone?"

"Cross my heart," Amy assured her.

But Jeanine would. There was no doubt in Amy's mind about that. And Amy had seen enough crime shows on TV to know that it wouldn't end with a bracelet. Jeanine would go on holding this over Simone's head. Whenever she wanted something from Simone, she'd threaten to tell the world about Simone's father.

What a despicable person Jeanine was. Amy recalled an incident back in first grade when Jeanine had taken great pleasure in pointing out how someone had wet his pants. She'd always been mean. Amy knew she shouldn't be surprised that Jeanine had sunk to blackmail. But it was still shocking.

She couldn't wait to tell Tasha at lunch—but then she remembered that she couldn't. She'd given Simone her word not to tell anyone. It was too bad. Amy would have loved to tell the world that she had absolute, definite, no-question-about-it confirmation of what she'd known for a long time. Jeanine Bryant was evil.

Instead she had to come up with something else to tell Tasha. Her friend would want to know what Amy had found out. Fortunately, when Amy arrived at their lunch table, Layne and Carrie were already there, so Tasha didn't bring up the subject of the bracelet. But as the others ate and chatted, Amy couldn't get her mind off what she'd learned. She began to wonder if this was how Jeanine was getting all her new stuff—by blackmailing students. But what kind of deep, dark secrets could so many students have?

"Earth to Amy."

She blinked. "Huh?"

Tasha was peering at her keenly. "You look like you're in outer space."

"Oh, I was just daydreaming," Amy said quickly. "What's up?"

"I was just telling you not to wait for me after school," Tasha said. "I've got a *Parkside News* meeting."

"I won't be leaving right after school either," Amy said. "I was late for first period so I've got detention."

The others expressed sympathy, but no one was surprised. Detention was a pretty common experience for students at Parkside. It was the standard punishment for everything from cutting class to running in the halls. It wasn't torture, but it wasn't any fun. For thirty minutes after school, you had to sit in a classroom and do nothing under the eyes of some poor teacher who'd been stuck with detention duty.

Of course, kids tried to get away with doing something, whether it was holding a book on their laps so they could read, or putting little earphones on to listen to music. In the detention classroom, Amy looked around to see if any of the other sufferers were doing anything interesting.

One boy in particular caught her attention. But this guy would catch *anyone's* attention. Amy had seen him around school and thought he was a ninth-grader. He was a big guy. Not fat, just big all over. He had a pierced eyebrow, a tattoo of a snake on his upper right arm, and a shaved head. Some kids, mainly guys, gazed at him in admiration. Personally, Amy thought he looked scary.

As they sat quietly, Amy noticed that he was shifting around restlessly in his seat. Then she saw him slip his hand surreptitiously into his pocket and withdraw a wallet. He extracted some bills, stuck them in an envelope, and sealed it. Then he wrote something on the envelope. With nothing else to do, Amy focused on the envelope until she could read the scrawled name. *Jeanine Bryant.*

Immediately Amy thought he must be another victim of Jeanine's blackmailing scheme, and she wondered what terrible secret Jeanine had unearthed about him.

This gave her something to ponder during the excruciating thirty minutes of doing nothing. A wide variety of criminal activities occupied her mind.

As soon as she was released, she went downstairs to the corridor outside the gym. Eric had basketball practice, and it should be just about the time that the coach gave the team a break. Sure enough, she only had to linger outside the gym doors for five minutes before the team came straggling out to line up at the water fountain.

"Amy, hi," Eric greeted her. "What are you doing here?"

She told him about staying for detention. "Do you know a big bald guy with a pierced eyebrow and a tattoo?"

"Sure," Eric said. "That's Dirt Sanders."

"Dirt?"

Eric grinned. "It's really Arthur, but hardly anyone knows that."

Amy wondered if a first name like that was a sufficient excuse for blackmail. "He looks scary," she said.

60

"That's how he tries to look," Eric told her. "He's in my PE class, and he's always practicing fierce expressions in the mirror. Poor guy, he's got a problem."

"What kind of problem?"

Eric lowered his voice. "He's got the locker next to mine. I saw this bottle of special shampoo for head lice in it. Don't tell anyone, okay? I don't want to embarrass the guy."

"Head lice," Amy repeated thoughtfully.

"I recognized the bottle 'cause I had lice in fifth grade," Eric said. "I'll bet that's why he had to shave his head. Of course, he lets everyone think he did it to look cool. It's not that big a deal having lice. Lots of kids get them, but I guess there are people who would tease him."

"Poor guy," Amy murmured. It was all falling into place. Somehow Jeanine had found out that Dirt Sanders had lice, and she was using that information to get money from him.

"Break's over!" the basketball coach bellowed, and Eric had to return to the gym.

But Amy remained in the corridor and thought about what she could do. Jeanine couldn't be allowed to get away with this. Amy decided to do a little threatening herself. She would go straight to Jeanine's house. There was always the possibility that Jeanine wouldn't be home, but dinnertime wasn't too far off. She'd be coming home eventually, and Amy would be waiting for her.

She didn't have to wait at all. Jeanine herself opened the front door.

Amy didn't bother with any greeting. "I have to talk to you."

Jeanine didn't appear in the least alarmed. In fact, she smiled. "Hi, Amy," she said in a voice that oozed sweetness. "Come on in."

Amy was caught off guard. It took her a second to collect herself. "No, thanks, I'd rather stay right here."

Jeanine continued to smile. "Whatever. Sorry I didn't have a chance to call you back last night. I was drowning in homework—you know what that's like. What did you want to talk about?"

There was no way Amy was going to let this phony charm put a damper on her anger. "I know what you've been up to, Jeanine."

Jeanine's smile didn't waver. There wasn't even the tiniest glimmer of concern in her eyes. "Oh, what am I up to, Amy?"

Her cocksure attitude was giving Amy an uneasy feeling. This wasn't how she'd envisioned the confrontation. She took a deep breath. "Blackmail. You've been blackmailing Simone Cusack, and Dirt Sanders, and who knows how many other people."

There was no reaction from Jeanine. None. She didn't act like she'd been wrongly accused. She didn't deny anything. She didn't even stop smiling. A cold shiver tickled Amy's spine, and she could feel goose bumps forming on her arms. She tried to ignore the sensations, and she kept talking.

"This has to stop, Jeanine. What you're doing is wrong. It's against the law."

Jeanine's response was eerily calm. "How are you going to stop me, Amy?"

This called for bringing out the big guns. "I'll tell Dr. Noble. I'll even go to the police. You'll be expelled and you'll be sent to some kind of juvenile reformatory."

She was striking no fear in Jeanine's heart. "You're not going to tell anyone anything, Amy. Because if you do, I'll tell everyone something about *you*."

A distant alarm went off in the back of Amy's head, but she ignored it. "What are you going to tell them, Jeanine? That I have cooties? Or warts on my toes? You don't scare me. Go right ahead and tell people whatever you want. I don't care."

Jeanine gazed at her thoughtfully. "Really? You don't care if I tell everyone that you're not a normal human being?"

For a second Amy couldn't breathe. "What—what did you say?"

"Oh, Amy, you know exactly what I'm talking about. You weren't born like a regular person. You were genetically engineered, in a laboratory. There are eleven other girls just like you. You're a clone."

Amy's head was spinning. She opened her mouth, but nothing came out.

Jeanine's smile broadened. "What's the matter, Amy Candler? You don't look like you're feeling so good. Maybe you'd better go home." And she shut the door in Amy's stunned face.

 **six**

Amy walked home in a daze. Her entire body felt as if it had been turned to stone. She was numb all over. She felt nothing. *This is a dream*, she told herself, *a nightmare, and I'm going to wake up any minute now.* But she didn't wake up, and as sensation returned to her body, fear permeated every pore of her skin.

This wasn't the first time in her life that she'd felt like she was in danger. In the past, she'd been forced to confront enemies bigger and stronger than she was. She'd been threatened with weapons that could do as much harm to her as they could to any ordinary person. She had saved the lives of others. There had been times when she had barely escaped with her own life.

No one was threatening her with bodily harm at this moment. And yet she was more frightened right now than she'd ever been before.

She opened the door of her house. "Mom?" she called out.

There was no response.

"Mom?" she said again, and she could hear her voice quavering. Then she remembered that her mother was teaching a late-afternoon class. She wouldn't be home for another hour.

Amy couldn't wait that long. She ran out of the house and across the lawn, praying that Tasha would be back from her meeting and Eric would be home from practice.

For once that day, she was in luck. Tasha opened the door. Like Amy, she was pretty good at reading expressions, and it didn't take more than a second for her to realize that something was terribly wrong.

"Amy! What happened?"

"Jeanine . . ." Amy practically choked on the name.

"What about Jeanine?"

It took even more effort to get the next words out. "She knows."

"She knows what?" Tasha said, and then she clapped a hand to her mouth. "Ohmigod."

Amy could see her own horror reflected in Tasha's eyes. For a second they were both motionless. Then Tasha held the door open wider and stepped aside for Amy to come in. As Amy moved stiffly into the living room, Tasha ran to the foot of the stairs. "Eric!" she shrieked, loudly enough to be heard over the sound of running water that came from the bathroom. "Come down! It's Amy!"

Eric must have heard the panic in his sister's voice. Seconds later he came tearing down the stairs, his wet hair spraying drops of water. He was still buttoning his shirt. "What's the matter?"

Amy turned to face him. "It's bad, Eric. It's very, very bad." She looked helplessly at Tasha, and her best friend took over.

"Jeanine found out about Amy."

For a moment Eric stared at her blankly. Then he realized what Tasha was saying, and he drew in his breath.

Just then Mrs. Morgan came in from the kitchen. Her eyes darted with concern among the three of them. "Kids, what's going on?"

Tasha was the first to recover. "Um, Amy wants

some help with her homework. We're going over there, okay?"

When they were safely in the Candler living room, they all sank down on the sofa. There was an eerie silence as they each tried to deal with the awfulness of the situation.

Then Eric got up and began to pace. "Are you sure she knows? I mean, how could she have found out?"

"I don't know," Amy said helplessly.

"Tell us exactly what happened," Tasha demanded.

"She said, she said . . ." Amy closed her eyes and recited from memory. " 'You weren't born like a regular person. You were genetically engineered in a laboratory. There are eleven other girls just like you. You're a clone.' "

Eric stared at her in confusion. "You mean she just walked up to you out of nowhere and said you were a clone?"

"Start from the beginning," Tasha urged.

Amy took a deep breath. "I found out that Jeanine's been blackmailing people. She finds out secrets about them, and then she threatens to tell everyone unless they give her what she wants."

Tasha let out a soft moan. "I should have guessed it was something like that. It's so very Jeanine."

"I told her to stop or I'd go to the police," Amy continued. "And she said no, I wouldn't, because then she'd tell everyone about me."

There were another few moments of silence as they all absorbed this. Then Eric spoke. "Well, one thing's for sure. You're not going to the police."

"And Jeanine will just go on blackmailing people," Tasha murmured.

Eric scowled at her. "Amy doesn't have any choice! If Jeanine starts spreading this story, it's going to reach the wrong people, and she's going to be in big trouble!" He turned his fearful eyes to Amy. "They'll come after you. They'll kidnap you, and take you away to some laboratory, and do experiments on you, and—"

"I know, I know!" Amy interrupted. "And it would be even worse than that."

"How could anything be worse than that?" Eric asked.

Amy stood up and began to pace the room. "It's not just me who's in danger, Eric. It's the whole world." She paused before a framed photograph of herself as a tiny baby in her mother's arms. "Think about it. Remember what I told you about, why my mother and the other scientists decided to terminate Project Crescent? They discovered that the organization funding their research wanted to develop a master race, a race of genetically enhanced people who would be stronger and smarter than all other people. And with that race of people, they could take over the world."

As her words sank in, Tasha sighed deeply. "I know. And that means Eric's right. You can't go to the police. Even if that means Jeanine continues to blackmail people."

"Right," Eric agreed. "Tell Jeanine you won't spill what you know about her to the authorities if she doesn't tell anyone what she knows about you."

Amy nodded slowly. "That might keep her mouth shut for now. But what about tomorrow? Or next week? Or next year?"

No one had an answer.

The sound of a car in the driveway summoned Amy to the window. "Here's my mother. Maybe she'll know what to do." But she had serious doubts that Nancy Candler would have a ready solution for this crisis.

And she was right. When her mother heard the whole story, she went deathly pale. Amy thought she would faint.

Her mother began to pace. "And you're sure she knows. She's not bluffing. You're sure you're not jumping to conclusions."

"She knows, Mom."

"But how? How could she know? I don't understand! How did this happen?"

Amy could only give her the same answer she'd given Eric and Tasha. "I don't know."

"Someone must have told her," Nancy said. "But who?"

No one bothered to attempt a response. They were all as much in the dark as she was.

Nancy stopped pacing. "Tasha, Eric . . . do you know anything?"

They both looked puzzled.

"Do you have any idea how this could have happened?" Nancy asked.

The implication of what she was asking hit Amy hard. "Mom! How can you ask them that?"

Now Tasha and Eric caught on. And they both looked utterly stunned. "Ms. Candler!" Tasha gasped. "We would never do anything like that!"

But Amy's mother persisted. "*Someone* told that girl. She couldn't have discovered this on her own."

Eric's tone was cold. "I'm not that stupid, Ms. Candler, and neither is Tasha. We're not disloyal, either."

Nancy was too distraught to realize how she had offended Amy's friends. "I'm going to call David," she said. "Maybe he'll know what to do." She ran upstairs.

An awkward tension filled the living room. Amy spoke apologetically. "My mother didn't mean that. She was just upset."

"We understand," Tasha replied stiffly. "But I think we'd better go now."

"I'll call you later," Eric said.

Alone, Amy tried to hear her mother's phone conversation. But Nancy wasn't saying much, and from the floor below, even Amy's excellent hearing couldn't make out Dr. Hopkins's words on the other end of the line.

She went into the kitchen to pick up the extension and listen in. She noticed the blinking light on the answering machine and hit the Play button.

There was the usual whirring rewinding sound, and then a familiar voice. "Hello, Amy, this is Jeanine. I have a favor to ask you. I've got a lot of homework, including a five-page essay on colonial settlements in Virginia, with footnotes and a bibliography. It's due on Friday, and I just don't have time to write it. Would you mind writing it for me? I think you'll be glad to do this favor for me. Because you know what could happen if you say no. Bye for now!"

There was a click, and no more messages. Amy stood very still and felt as if an ice-cold knife had been plunged into her back. The fear she'd expressed to Tasha and Eric had just been confirmed.

Keeping her mouth shut about the blackmail wouldn't be enough to satisfy Jeanine.

seven

In her next-to-last period on Wednesday, Amy sat in the classroom and tried to look as if she was paying attention, but her mind was a million miles away. She had been like this all day. She couldn't concentrate. She couldn't listen. Her mind just kept going over the same sequence of events: Jeanine's announcement, the reaction of Amy's friends and her mother, the message on the answering machine.

And her mother's advice to her.

"I talked to David and he agrees with me," Nancy had told Amy. "There's only one thing for you to do. You have to talk to Jeanine and tell her how very, very important it is that she keep this secret. You've got to make her realize how serious your situation is. She has to understand that this is no childish game. She has to know that the future of humanity is at stake!"

Amy recalled her own response: "Jeanine doesn't care about the future of humanity, Mom. She only cares about Jeanine Bryant."

And her mother's reply: "Good heavens, Amy, she can't be that bad. She's a person, she's not a monster!"

But Amy wasn't so sure about that. That very morning, in homeroom, she'd tried to follow her mother's directions. "I have to talk to you," she'd told Jeanine.

Surrounded by her friends, Jeanine had smiled. "What about?" she'd asked innocently.

"It's personal," Amy replied.

"Well, no offense, Amy, but I really don't want to know any more personal stuff about you. I know enough already."

Amy could still see the curious expressions on Jeanine's friends' faces. And she knew Jeanine was sending her a message. *All I have to do, Amy, is tell these friends and it will be all over the school in five minutes.*

Amy hadn't pleaded further. What good would it have done? She knew what Jeanine was all about. She might as well plead with a cloud not to rain on her head. Nothing would convince Jeanine to do the right thing.

Amy would be writing an essay on colonial settlements in Virginia. There would be another essay after that, and another, and another. The demands would go beyond schoolwork. Amy would be turning over her allowance, performing Jeanine's chores, and maybe even stealing for her, or hurting someone, or even worse. . . . Suddenly Amy felt like she was about to throw up.

"Amy?"

She looked up. The teacher was gazing at her with concern. "Are you all right?"

Amy didn't even try to control the tremor in her voice. "Actually, I'm not feeling very well." The classmates sitting around her looked at her in alarm and began edging their desks away from hers.

"I think you should go to the clinic," the teacher said. She wrote out a pass and handed it to Amy. Amy gathered her things and left the room.

But once she was in the hall, she knew she wasn't going to the clinic. She knew she wasn't really sick, and the only reason to go to the clinic would be to lie down and maybe sleep. Sleep, and not think. It was tempting. But it would be like admitting defeat. And she wasn't ready for that, not yet.

It wasn't hard to find Jeanine's classroom. Amy hurried up and down the halls, waving her pass at hall monitors and peeking through the window of every door she passed. But when she located the classroom, she wasn't sure what to do next. Should she try the same method she'd used to get Simone out of class? Tell the teacher Jeanine was needed for a project?

But this wasn't a study hall, so it was very unlikely that the teacher would excuse Jeanine. Besides, what made Amy think Jeanine would agree to leave a classroom with her?

Amy ripped a blank piece of paper out of her notebook and scrawled a message on it. *Jeanine. Get a bathroom pass and meet me on the landing of the west wing stairs. Now.* She underlined the *Now* three times. She scribbled her name and folded the paper again and again to note-passing size.

But how was she going to get the note to Jeanine?

"Amy?"

She turned to see Layne standing behind her, a bathroom pass in her hand. "Layne, are you in this class?" Amy asked. And when Layne nodded, Amy said, "Could you pass this note to Jeanine?"

Layne looked at her oddly. "Since when are you and Jeanine buddies?"

Amy was totally unable to come up with a response,

but fortunately Layne didn't demand an explanation. She took the note from Amy and went into the classroom.

Looking through the window, Amy saw the teacher glance toward the door. Amy didn't dare wait to watch Layne give the note to Jeanine. She took off and went down the hall to the west wing stairs.

In the silence of the stairwell, she huddled on the landing between the two floors and waited. Would Layne get the note to Jeanine? Would Jeanine come? If she knew the extent of Amy's physical strength, she might be afraid to meet her alone like this.

And if Jeanine did come, what would Amy say to her? Despite what her mother had said, she truly doubted that Jeanine would listen to a rational explanation. But she had to tell her mother that she'd tried. In her mind she began to compose a heartfelt argument.

She hadn't gotten far in her mental composition when the door leading to the stairwell opened and Jeanine appeared. Sauntering up the dozen stairs to the landing, she didn't look the least bit worried. Only a little annoyed.

"Couldn't this wait till after school?" she asked. "I'll give you the essay assignment then."

"I'm not going to do your essay, Jeanine," Amy said. Quickly she added, "But I won't go to the police either. I'll keep your secret if you'll keep mine."

Jeanine sighed in exasperation. "Get real, Amy. Your secret's a lot bigger than mine. I'm in charge here. I make the rules. Who's going to be interested in my secret besides the principal and a few parents? But I bet the whole world would love to know about you."

So she did understand the significance of Amy's secret. And it didn't make any difference at all.

"Tell me what you want," Amy said. "How about if I resign from student council? I could even say that my friends stuffed the ballot box and you were the real winner of the election."

Jeanine contemplated the proposal. But any hope Amy might have felt was dashed when that evil smile reappeared. "Gee, that hadn't even occurred to me. It's not a bad idea. But it won't be enough." She eyed Amy thoughtfully. "You really don't want your secret to get out, do you? Just out of curiosity, what's your IQ? And exactly how strong are you? I need to know, Amy, because you're going to be working for me, and I want to figure out the best ways I can use you."

"Jeanine, *please*," Amy implored. "You can't, you *can't* let anyone know about me!"

"I won't," Jeanine replied. "As long as you do what I tell you to do."

"I won't be your slave," Amy said.

"Amy, have you ever heard of the *National Star*?"

Amy had. It was one of those tabloid newspapers that were stuffed into the racks at supermarket check-out counters. "What about it?"

"They pay for news stories," Jeanine said. "The more sensational the story, the more dough they cough up. It says so right on the front page. There's this 800 number you can call if you know juicy information other people would die to find out. I'll bet they'd pay a lot to discover that there's a real live clone at Parkside Middle School. They'd send reporters, and then television cameras, and pretty soon the whole world would know about Amy Candler."

Amy could feel her knees going weak. "You can't," she whispered.

"I can," Jeanine said. "And I will. If you don't obey me." And then she started to laugh. Like a witch, she cackled with glee. It was all Amy could do not to rush at her and beat her to a pulp. Instead, she turned away and fled up the stairs to the next floor.

In the hall a monitor spotted her. "Hey, what are you doing?"

She spotted a girls' rest room and ran in. She was lucky that this monitor happened to be a boy and couldn't follow her.

Inside the rest room she walked in circles, trying to control the panic that was rising inside her. What to do, what to do . . . there was nothing to do. Absolutely nothing. She would now and forevermore be at Jeanine's mercy. Or at the mercy of people even more dangerous. What to do, what to do . . .

Even in her panic, and through the thick door of the rest room, her ears picked up a sound. It was a shriek. No, more like a scream. Then there was a loud, dull thump.

Amy hurried out of the rest room and ran back into the stairwell. She rushed down one flight. On the landing, she gasped. A body lay at the bottom of the stairs. She flew down the rest of the stairs and bent over it.

Other people appeared in the stairwell, and Amy looked up. She saw her homeroom teacher, Ms. Weller, and Madame Duquesne, her French teacher, and the custodian, Mr. Nevins. A couple of hall monitors were there too.

They were all looking down at the crumpled body of Jeanine Bryant.

e8ight

The next few moments were a blur. The crowd in the stairwell increased, and as each new person arrived, the fresh shrieks of horror attracted even more people. Shouts of "Don't move her" and "Call nine one one" came from all directions. In vain, teachers were ordering students to return to their classrooms immediately. Eventually, when they were threatened with a zillion demerits, the students began to disperse.

Back in her own classroom, Amy joined the others at the window that faced the school parking lot. The teacher was at the window too, not even trying to get them back into their seats. The wail of a siren filled the air, and it grew louder as the ambulance approached the school. Students were yakking loudly, wanting to know what had happened.

Amy, of course, knew what was going on, but she didn't respond to the questions. For some reason she was afraid to speak. She was afraid that her voice might betray her. She was afraid that her tone might reveal feelings that went beyond innocent distress.

She was in a state of shock. One minute Jeanine had been alive, and the next minute . . . She couldn't bring herself to even think the word.

In the midst of all the hubbub, the sound of the bell told them it was time to change classes. Then the intercom came on, telling everyone to remain where they were and ignore all bells. But by that time some kids had left and others had already arrived for their next class. Amy went out into the hall, where the scene was chaos as students tried to figure out what to do, where to go, and why all this was happening. Someone—it sounded like Linda Riviera—was sobbing loudly.

"She's dead! Jeanine's dead!"

But Jeanine wasn't dead. "She's at Northside Hospital," Tasha told Amy when she called her at home later that afternoon. "My mother talked to some friend of

Mrs. Bryant. She said Jeanine's in extremely critical condition."

"She's not dead," Amy murmured.

"No, not yet," Tasha said.

"Tasha!"

"What?"

"You sound so—so cruel!"

"I'm just being practical," Tasha said. "When a person is in extremely critical condition, there's a strong possibility they might die."

"I guess."

"It's true. I'm not making it up," Tasha replied. "That's even what Layne Hunter told me, and she's a candy striper. That's almost like being a nurse."

"It is *not*," Amy said sharply. "A candy striper is a volunteer, for crying out loud. She gives out magazines and stuff to patients. She doesn't do anything medical, like a nurse."

Tasha didn't like her tone. "Okay, okay, don't bite my head off! Hey, what's *your* problem? It's not like Jeanine was a friend of yours!"

Amy had some difficulty responding to that. "I know, but it's still terrible when anyone has an accident. Even someone as awful as Jeanine. I wouldn't want her to *die*."

Somehow she knew what Tasha would say next. "If she did, it would certainly solve your problem."

"Oh, Tasha," Amy said weakly. "Let's not talk about that, okay?"

The second she hung up the phone, it rang again and she snatched it up. "Hello?"

Her mother's voice came out in a rush of relief. "Oh, honey, thank goodness you're okay. I just heard that a girl was seriously hurt at Parkside Middle School."

"It wasn't me," Amy assured her. "I'm fine."

"Are you sure?" her mother asked anxiously. "I'm supposed to go to a faculty reception here at the university this evening. But if you're feeling upset, I can come home."

"You don't have to," Amy said again. "I really am fine. Have a nice time at the reception."

She half listened to her mother's usual instructions about not opening the door to strangers, and to call Monica Jackson if there were any problems. It wasn't until she hung up the phone that she realized her mother hadn't asked who the injured girl was. Her mother had no doubt been so relieved to know that it wasn't Amy that she probably wasn't thinking about anything else.

Amy was glad her mother hadn't asked. She was too

confused to discuss her feelings about Jeanine with anyone, even her mother. She went to bed early, before her mother got home from the reception, to avoid any questions.

She couldn't avoid them in the morning, though. Nancy's first question at breakfast was about the identity of the girl who'd been hurt. Amy knew there was no point in beating around the bush; her mother would learn who it was eventually.

"Jeanine Bryant. She fell down some stairs."

"Jeanine? Amy, isn't she the one who—"

"Yes," Amy said before her mother could finish the question.

Nancy was quiet for a moment. "Did you do what we discussed, Amy? Did you talk with her?"

Amy hesitated. "Yes," she said finally. "Sort of." And then, fortunately, Tasha and Eric appeared at the door, so there was no more time to talk about it.

As the friends walked to school, Tasha reported all the latest news from Layne. "Jeanine smashed her head," Tasha said. "There are broken bones too, but the head's the most serious thing. There might be brain damage."

Amy shuddered. "That's horrible."

"Layne got a peek at her," Tasha went on. "She said

Jeanine's all hooked up to tubes and machines. Layne says the last time she saw someone hooked up to so much stuff, they died the next day."

"Can we *not* talk about this, *please*?" Amy asked.

"Yeah, Tasha," Eric echoed. "You sound like you don't care if the girl lives or dies."

"I don't know how I feel," Tasha said honestly. "Amy, *you* must be feeling *really* weird. You can't tell me it wouldn't be a relief if she died."

"Don't say that," Amy begged. "It makes me feel so guilty!"

Eric put a comforting arm around her shoulder. "There's no reason for you to feel guilty. Hey, you know what would be perfect? If she makes a complete recovery with just a tiny bit of brain damage to her memory. So she forgets what she knows about Amy."

"That *would* be good," Amy admitted. "But I'd still like to know *how* she found out about me."

"I hope you're not thinking what your mother was thinking," Tasha said a little huffily.

"Of course not," Amy quickly assured her. "And I know my mother didn't mean to sound like she was accusing you."

"Sure, she was just upset," Eric said. Tasha didn't look completely mollified, but she let the subject drop.

At school, Linda Riviera was holding court on the steps that led to the main entrance. As Jeanine's best friend, she was expected to have the latest information. Amy, Tasha, and Eric moved to the edge of the group that surrounded her and listened in.

"She's in a coma," Linda reported, and the break in her voice told Amy that as shallow and dreary as Linda was, at least she was sincere in her distress. "She hasn't regained consciousness at all. The doctors don't know if she'll survive."

A boy Amy recognized as a hall monitor spoke. "Man, when I saw her at the bottom of the stairs yesterday, I thought she was dead."

"Were you the first one on the scene?" someone asked.

"No, this other girl beat me to her . . . hey, there she is!"

Suddenly all eyes were on Amy. She felt her face redden. "I was in the third-floor rest room," she told them. "I heard her scream."

"Was she conscious when you got to her?" a boy asked.

"No."

Linda spoke. "How about while she was falling? Was she conscious then?"

"I didn't see her fall, Linda," Amy replied.

Linda's eyes narrowed to tiny little slits. "Are you sure?"

Amy stared at her. "What do you mean by that?"

"I'm thinking that maybe Jeanine didn't fall," Linda said. "Maybe she was pushed."

Everyone gasped.

"Linda!" Amy exclaimed. "Are you accusing *me* of pushing Jeanine down the stairs?"

"Well, you hated her," Linda declared hotly.

Amy wanted to point out that lots of people hated Jeanine, but she stopped herself—after all, Jeanine was in a coma and her best friend was terribly upset. Fortunately, Tasha and Eric were there to come to Amy's defense.

"Linda!" Tasha shouted. "Amy would *never* do anything like that and you know it!"

"Yeah, try to think before you talk, Linda!" Eric barked.

Amy was gratified to hear other kids making the same kind of comment. It was almost time for the bell, so the group broke up and moved inside the building. Eric went off to join his pals, and Amy and Tasha walked to their lockers.

"How could Linda even *think* I would deliberately push Jeanine down the stairs?" Amy marveled.

Tasha had the answer to that. "Because she's not the brightest crayon in the box and she's Jeanine's best friend. You know she'd love to find a way to blame this on you."

"But it was an accident," Amy protested. "She can't blame anyone! Tasha, what if she goes around spreading rumors that I pushed Jeanine down the stairs?"

Tasha brushed that aside. "No one would believe her."

Amy knew that what Tasha said was true. After all, Amy had a good reputation at Parkside. No one would ever think she could be violent.

Even so, she had the prickly sensation that a couple of kids looked at her strangely when she entered her homeroom. But surely that was just her imagination.

The bell rang, and Ms. Weller took the roll. Then the intercom came on. "Please give your complete attention to the morning announcements," rang out the strong, commanding voice of Dr. Noble, and everyone turned toward the gray box on the wall.

"We know that you are all very concerned about Jeanine Bryant," Dr. Noble said. "I spoke with her doctor this morning, and there is no change in her condition. She is still in the intensive care unit of Northside Hospital. I will let you all know if I receive any more information later today."

The principal went on to make the usual announcements about club meetings and athletic events. She asked for students to bring in any old coats they might have for a clothing drive.

Amy was jotting down a note to check her closet at home when she heard her own name. "Would Amy Candler please come to the office immediately?"

She almost dropped her pencil. The last time anyone had been called to the office over the intercom was when a student's father had suddenly died. She could feel her heart rate accelerate as she leaped out of her seat, accepted a pass from Ms. Weller, and ran out the classroom door. It took her less than a minute to get to the office, but she was out of breath from panic. Thank goodness she didn't have to wait.

"Dr. Noble will see you now," the secretary told her, and Amy went into the principal's office. The moment she saw the principal, she felt better. Dr. Noble looked serious, but she smiled.

"Good morning, Amy," she said. "I've called you in to find out what you know about this." Dr. Noble handed her an unfolded sheet of paper. Amy recognized it immediately and held her breath as she silently read the familiar words.

Jeanine. Get a bathroom pass and meet me on the landing of the west wing stairs. Now. Amy.

"Did you write that note?" Dr. Noble asked.

"Yes," Amy whispered.

"It was found on Jeanine's desk by the custodian this morning," the principal continued. "Was Jeanine supposed to meet you on the landing of the west wing stairs yesterday?"

"Yes," Amy whispered again.

"But when you got there, she was lying at the bottom of the stairs," Dr. Noble said.

Amy hesitated. She *could* say yes to that, in truth. The second time she had gone into the stairwell, Jeanine had been lying there. Being a basically honest person could be a real drag sometimes.

"I met her before she fell," Amy confessed. "And we talked. Then I went to the rest room on the third floor. That's when I heard her fall."

"Did you see anyone else around?"

Amy shook her head.

"No one was running from the scene?"

Amy shook her head again.

"All right. That will be all, Amy. You can go back to class now."

She hadn't asked why Amy had wanted to meet with Jeanine. But Amy was still holding her breath as she put her hand on the doorknob.

"And Amy?"

She thought her heart would stop. "Yes, Dr. Noble?"

"Passing notes is not appropriate behavior. Especially when you're not in the same class, which means you had to get a pass to leave your own class."

"Yes, Dr. Noble. I'm sorry, I won't do it again."

And then she was free. Once outside the office, she leaned against the wall and closed her eyes for a moment. When she opened them, she noticed Mr. Nevins, the custodian, looking at her oddly as he put a box of envelopes in a cabinet. "You okay?" he asked gruffly.

Amy nodded. Then she remembered what Dr. Noble had said about the custodian's finding the note. Mr. Nevins was probably thinking that she'd had something to do with Jeanine's accident. She ran out into the hall and back to homeroom.

She didn't say a word to anyone about the meeting with Dr. Noble. She would have liked to share the story with Tasha at lunch, but Layne and Carrie sat with them, and Amy didn't want people asking her why she had passed a note to Jeanine.

Naturally, the conversation pretty much revolved around the injured girl. "I'm going to try to see her this afternoon," Carrie declared.

"She's not allowed any visitors," Layne told her.

"Yeah, but maybe some flowers will be delivered for her and I can put them in her room," Carrie said. "At least then I might get a look at her."

"Are you a candy striper too?" Tasha asked.

Carrie nodded. "A bunch of us went through the training last month. Me and Layne, Heather Graves, Jane Fiorello, Simone Cusack . . ."

"We should send flowers," Amy said to Tasha.

"It's very expensive to have them delivered," Layne warned her. "It's a lot cheaper if you buy the flowers and take them to the hospital yourself."

Later, after school, Tasha asked Amy if she was serious about sending flowers. Amy nodded. "I'm feeling even worse about her now." She told Tasha and Eric about her meeting with Dr. Noble.

"It sounds like they think someone pushed her," Eric said.

"Maybe," Amy agreed.

"Let me get this straight," Tasha said. "You were actually *with* Jeanine in the stairwell before she fell?"

"My mom wanted me to try to talk with her. And now I'm thinking that if I hadn't gotten angry and stormed off, I would have been able to save her." She realized that both Eric and Tasha were looking at her as if she'd just lost her mind.

"Well, I would have!" she declared firmly. "And so would you. Come on, guys, let's go buy some flowers and bring them to the hospital."

"Okay, Saint Amy," Eric said cheerfully. "I guess it's about time for me to do my once-a-year good deed."

Northside Hospital was close to their school, which was why the ambulance had brought Jeanine there. There was a gift store on the ground floor, where they pooled their money and bought a bouquet. The receptionist at the information desk told them that Jeanine was on the third floor and directed them to the elevator. As the elevator took them up, Tasha looked at the bouquet and sighed. "What a waste of pretty flowers."

"Tasha!" Amy exclaimed reprovingly.

"Well, if Jeanine's in a coma, she won't even know they're in the room!"

"Maybe she's out of her coma now," Eric said.

"Yeah, maybe," Amy said, and she wondered if she was the only one who could hear the quiver in her voice.

But according to the clerk at the nurses' station on the third floor, there was no change in Jeanine's condition, so she wasn't allowed any visitors. "One of our candy stripers will put the flowers in her room," the clerk told them. "Maybe they'll be the first thing she sees when she comes out of her coma."

"Do you think she'll come out of the coma?" Tasha asked.

The clerk shrugged. "I'm just the clerk—I don't know. But I like to think positive."

"Out of the way," a voice muttered. It was coming from behind a huge rolling cart on which stacks of towels obscured the speaker.

"That's not polite," the clerk scolded. "Around here, we say 'Excuse me.' "

The person wheeling the cart didn't reply, but as he passed them Eric gave a yelp of recognition. "Yo, Dirt!"

"Not in *this* hospital!" the clerk declared haughtily. But the guy behind the cart gave Eric a salute.

"Hey, man."

Now Amy too could see the pierced, tattooed bald guy, another one of Jeanine's victims. She smiled at him, and he responded with a grimace that might have been his version of a smile.

"You working here?" Eric asked.

"Sort of," Dirt replied. "Community service. I got picked up driving my old man's car without a license. They gave me a choice, a week in jail or six months of pushing stuff around here."

"Well, take it easy," Eric said, and Dirt moved on with his towels. To Amy, Eric whispered, "I guess head lice isn't the only problem this guy has."

"There are Mr. and Mrs. Bryant," Tasha pointed out.

Amy watched the couple talking to a man in a long white coat. Then Mrs. Bryant came over to the nurses' station. "Hello, Mrs. Bryant," the clerk said. "These young people just brought flowers for Jeanine."

"That's nice," Mrs. Bryant said. She looked at Amy, Eric, and Tasha vaguely. Amy had always thought Jeanine's mother was an awful snob, but she had to feel sorry for her now.

"I hope Jeanine gets better real soon, Mrs. Bryant," she said.

Mrs. Bryant focused on her. "You're the Candler girl. The one who used to be in Jeanine's gymnastics class."

"That's me," Amy said brightly.

Mrs. Bryant frowned. "But you're not one of Jeanine's good friends, are you?"

Amy managed a thin smile. "Well, we're in homeroom together. . . ." Mrs. Bryant barely nodded before she rejoined her husband and the doctor. "Can we go now?" Amy whispered to Eric and Tasha.

They were happy to. It was while they were waiting for the elevator that Eric recognized someone else from Parkside. "Isn't that Mr. Nevins, the custodian?"

"Or his identical twin brother," Tasha said.

But it *was* Mr. Nevins, and he grunted in their direction to show he'd recognized them. He was wearing the same kind of overalls he wore at Parkside, but these had NORTHSIDE HOSPITAL written on the pocket.

"You work here, Mr. Nevins?" Eric asked politely.

The man nodded. "I need two jobs just to make a living," he said.

"That must be tough," Eric replied.

"Yeah, it is." Mr. Nevins shrugged. "At least the school isn't as depressing as this place." He frowned and moved on.

"See you at school," Eric shouted after him. He turned to Amy and Tasha. "I guess Parkside doesn't pay him a great salary."

Amy had to smile. "Eric, it's not your fault Mr. Nevins needs more money than our school pays him."

"I know," Eric said. Then he looked at her pointedly. "Just like it's not your fault that Jeanine is in the hospital."

Eric was right, of course, and Amy just had to keep reminding herself of that. Just because she hated Jeanine, that didn't make her responsible for the girl's misfortune.

Of course, that wasn't what Linda Riviera thought. . . .

nine

"I call this meeting of the Parkside Middle School student council to order." As Cliff Fields rapped his gavel on the desk on Monday morning, Amy leaned forward and tried to think positively. Maybe the previous week's boring meeting had been a fluke.

But no such luck. It looked like this meeting was going to be equally dull. The secretary read the past week's minutes, the vice president called the roll, the treasurer gave his report. Then the president called for the announcements.

Assistant Principal Carroll made the first announcement. "I must tell you all that the theft of school supplies and equipment has continued and is actually getting worse. We are now missing four computers, seven electronic staple guns, camera equipment, a laser printer—practically everything that isn't nailed down is disappearing! We must find out who is responsible for this! If anyone knows anything, please get in touch with the main office immediately."

Amy gazed around the room. No one looked even remotely interested.

Carrie had an announcement to make. "I was at Northside Hospital yesterday," she reported. "And I saw Jeanine Bryant. She's still in a coma and is being fed through a tube. But she's in a private room now, and she can have visitors for short periods, one at a time."

"What's the point of visiting if she's in a coma?" someone asked. "She won't even know the person's there."

"Some doctors think that people in comas can hear, and that a familiar voice might help bring them out of the coma," Carrie told them.

Once the announcements were finished, the meeting moved swiftly. There was no old business and no new business, and the vote to adjourn was unanimous.

Amy waited for Carrie at the door. "Do doctors really think a person in a coma can hear stuff?" she asked.

"That's what the nurses told me," Carrie replied.

"Last year I remember seeing a news show about a boy who was in a coma, and his family visited him in his hospital room. His father turned on the TV just as the boy's favorite show started. When the theme music of the show came on, the boy woke up!"

"Wow," Amy marveled.

"So I guess you won't be visiting Jeanine," Carrie continued.

Amy was puzzled. "Why not?"

"She dumped a milk shake on your head, remember? You'll be happy if she stays in a coma forever!"

Carrie might have been kidding around, but Amy wasn't sure. And if Carrie was joking, Amy was not amused. "Carrie, that's not true! I'll admit that I don't like Jeanine, but I hope she gets better."

"Hi, guys." Simone was sauntering toward them. "What's up?"

"Student council meeting," Carrie said. "Weren't you supposed to be working at the hospital yesterday? I didn't see you."

"I changed shifts with Layne," Simone replied. "I'm going there after school today. Did you get to see Jeanine?"

Carrie nodded. "She's in a private room now, on the fifth floor." Glancing around, she lowered her voice. "Have you heard the rumors?"

"What rumors?" Simone asked.

"People are saying that Jeanine didn't just fall down those stairs. They're saying she was pushed."

"That's crazy!" Amy exclaimed. "Who would do something like that?"

Simone shrugged. "Well, if anyone had a reason, it would be you."

Amy's mouth fell open. Surely Simone wasn't serious! *She* had almost as much reason to dislike Jeanine as Amy had. As she thought about this, Amy's eyes went automatically to Simone's wrist. She blinked twice to make sure she was seeing what she thought she was seeing.

Simone was wearing the silver-and-turquoise bracelet her cousin had sent for her birthday.

"Bell's about to ring," Carrie announced. The girls split up, and as Amy went into her homeroom, her mind was occupied with two confusing thoughts. The first: How had Simone gotten her bracelet back from Jeanine? The second: Did people really think she hated Jeanine so much that she would push her down a flight of stairs?

That second notion stayed with her all day. "I keep getting the feeling people are looking at me funny," she confided in Tasha at lunch. Layne and Carrie hadn't joined them, and they were alone.

"Why?" Tasha asked.

"Have you heard the rumors about someone *pushing* Jeanine down the stairs?"

Tasha nodded. "In my last class, someone said she heard Jeanine was hit on the head with something heavy, like a brick or a baseball bat."

Amy shook her head in amazement. "It's awful how fast rumors spread."

But Tasha looked thoughtful. "If she was hit on the head first, it would explain why she was so seriously injured. People fall down stairs all the time and they don't end up in a coma."

"Are you saying someone was trying to kill her?" Amy asked.

"An awful lot of people hate her," Tasha said. "Picture this. You're standing on a stairwell with Jeanine. She says something really terrible. You've got a heavy object in your hand. No one else is around. You get so angry, you can't stop yourself, you hit her with the object, and she falls down the stairs."

Amy stared at her friend. "Why do you keep saying *you* like you're talking about me?"

"Don't be silly, I'm just using *you* to mean anyone," Tasha replied.

Amy knew that was true. But for the remainder of

the day, she continued to feel that people were looking at her strangely. And she became less sure that it was all in her imagination.

Maybe that was why she felt she absolutely had to go to the hospital that afternoon. She wanted to show everyone that she sincerely hoped Jeanine would come out of her coma.

Eric couldn't go with her—he had basketball practice. And Tasha declined. "We already brought her flowers," she said. "I'd feel like a total hypocrite if I went again. I mean, what would I say to her? 'Hi, Jeanine, I still don't like you, and I never will, but I hope you get better so I can go on not liking you'?"

"I know," Amy said. "I don't blame you for feeling like that. But I have to go."

"Why?"

Amy couldn't say "So people won't think I pushed Jeanine down the stairs." It would sound paranoid. "I just feel like I have to go," she said lamely. How could she explain to Tasha when she wasn't even sure of the real reason herself?

So she went alone to Northside Hospital. She remembered what Carrie had said about Jeanine being in a private room now, and she took the elevator to the fifth floor. When the elevator doors opened, she found herself face-to-face with a six-foot stack of linens on a cart.

She moved to the left to get around the cart, but the cart moved in the same direction, preventing her from leaving the elevator. She edged to the right, but once again the cart followed her, blocking her way. She moved quickly back to the left side, but the cart moved that way too. And then it began to come forward, into the elevator, directly toward her.

For one terrible moment she thought the cart would crush her against the back wall of the elevator. Immediately she raised her arms to stop it, and she yelled, "Hey, watch out!"

The cart stopped, and a figure came around the linens from the other end. It was Dirt Sanders. "Sorry," he muttered as he moved the cart so she could get out. Amy tried to smile to show that he was forgiven. But Dirt didn't smile back, and he didn't look the least bit sorry.

Amy didn't know what to make of Dirt's attitude, but she pushed him out of her head as she strode purposefully toward the nurses' station. "Room five oh five," the nurse told her. "But you can only stay a few minutes."

"Okay," Amy agreed, and started down the hall. Before

she could reach the door, it opened. Dressed in her candy striper's uniform and pushing a cart covered with magazines, Simone emerged from Jeanine's room. She looked startled to see Amy.

"What are you doing here?"

"I came to see Jeanine! Carrie said talking to her might bring her out of her coma."

"Suit yourself," Simone said. "I'll bet it won't work." As she started to move on, Amy glanced at her wrist.

"You're not wearing your bracelet," she blurted out. "The silver-and-turquoise bracelet your cousin sent you. You had it on this morning at school."

"We're not allowed to wear jewelry with our uniforms," Simone answered, clearly annoyed. Quickly she pushed the cart through the open door of the next room.

Amy went on into Jeanine's room. The light was dim, and she had to move close to the bed to get a good look at the injured girl.

It's a good thing Jeanine can't see herself, Amy thought. She'd be really upset. The heavy white bandages completely covered her head, and there were dark bruises on her face. She lay very, very still. A machine was attached to her by a thin cable on one side, and by her other side, an IV bag hung from a pole. A tube coming from the bag disappeared under the sheet that covered her.

It was going to be weird, talking to this unconscious figure. But Amy gave it a try. "Hello, Jeanine, this is Amy. I hope you're not feeling too awful. I'm sure it isn't nice to be in a coma, but at least maybe it doesn't hurt. I mean, I hope you don't feel any pain."

This wasn't so bad. It was actually easier talking to an unconscious Jeanine than a conscious one. But Amy knew she wouldn't be allowed to stay long, so she had to get to the point.

"Jeanine, I'm also hoping that if you come out of this—I mean, *when* you come out of this—you'll keep my secret. It's awfully important that no one finds out that I'm genetically engineered. I know you don't care about what happens to *me,* but there are a lot of other people who could suffer. And you don't really want me to be your slave. Wouldn't you rather be friends? I know we don't get along, but we could try, and then maybe—"

She didn't get any farther with her plea. The door opened. "Who's in here?" a voice asked sharply. Amy turned to see Jeanine's mother standing in the doorway. Linda Riviera was just behind her.

"It's me, Amy Candler, Mrs. Bryant," Amy said. "I was told it's a good idea to talk to people in a coma."

Mrs. Bryant pushed her out of the way and looked down at Jeanine. She lifted the sheet that covered her daughter.

And then she screamed.

"Her feeding tube's out! Get the nurse, get a doctor, hurry!"

Amy ran out the door, but Linda had already flagged down a nurse, who ran into the room. Amy remained in the hallway with Linda, who was staring at her in alarm.

"What did you *do* to her?" Linda asked.

Amy looked at her in bewilderment. "Me? I didn't do anything. I was just talking to her."

The door opened, and the nurse and Mrs. Bryant emerged. "She'll be all right; we caught it in time," the nurse was saying. "I don't know how that could have happened. I suppose she could have pulled it out in her sleep, but that's not common."

"It was *her*!" Linda shrieked, pointing at Amy. "She pulled the tube out of Jeanine's arm!"

Amy gasped. "I did *not*!"

"She hates Jeanine," Linda went on in a shrill voice. "She's the one who pushed her down the stairs in the first place! She wants to kill her!"

"Linda, that's not true!" Amy cried out.

"Keep your voices down," the nurse warned them. She looked long and hard at Amy.

Mrs. Bryant's expression was even harder, and her eyes shot sparks in Amy's direction. "Get out of here," she said through her teeth. "Get away from my daughter, and if I ever see you here again, I'll have you arrested. Do you hear me? Get out!"

Amy fled.

ten 10

Amy knew something was wrong as soon as she opened her front door the next morning. "Tasha, you're early!" she said. "Where's Eric?"

Tasha seemed nervous. "I need to talk to you alone. Can we go now?"

"Sure," Amy said. She yelled goodbye to her mother, grabbed her jacket and bag, and joined Tasha outside. "What's up? I have something to tell you too. I tried to call you last night but you weren't home."

"I was at Layne's," Tasha said. Her voice wasn't normal, and Amy looked at her curiously.

"What's the matter?"

"You tell me your news first," Tasha urged.

"I went to the hospital to see Jeanine after school yesterday," Amy told her. "You wouldn't believe what happened to me!"

"Yes, I would," Tasha said.

"Huh?"

"I already know about it," Tasha told her. "Simone came over to Layne's after her candy striper shift. She told us how Jeanine's tube had been pulled out and that she could have died."

"Did she tell you that Linda and Mrs. Bryant accused *me* of pulling the tube?"

Tasha nodded.

"Can this get any weirder?" Amy demanded. "First I'm accused of being happy that Jeanine fell down the stairs. Then I'm accused of pushing her down the stairs. And now they're saying I pulled out her feeding tube!"

"It's pretty weird," Tasha admitted. After a moment she asked, "Were you alone with Jeanine in the hospital room?"

"Yeah. They only let her have one visitor at a time."

"You were alone with her when you met her in the stairwell last week too, right?"

Amy stared at her. "What are you getting at?"

Their walk had slowed, and now Tasha stopped. "Amy . . ."

"What?"

Tasha turned and faced her. "You know I'm your best friend, right?"

"Right."

"And you know you can tell me anything, *anything*, and I'll always believe you, and I'll never be angry at you, no matter what you tell me."

"Sure," Amy said. "I know that."

Tasha seemed to be choosing her words carefully. "Amy . . . is there something you want to tell me?"

Totally bewildered, Amy asked, "Tell you about what?"

"About Jeanine."

Amy stepped back. "Tasha!" She drew in her breath. "Tasha, ohmigod, you don't think *I* did anything to hurt Jeanine, do you?"

"Of course not," Tasha said quickly. Too quickly. "Not . . . on purpose," she added. "But people are talking about you, Amy."

Aghast, Amy asked, "*What* people? Someone besides Linda?"

Miserably Tasha nodded. "Simone, and Layne, and

Carrie . . . well, you know how fast stories spread at Parkside."

Amy stood there, unable to speak, knowing all too well the speed of the rumor mill in middle school.

Now Tasha was speaking very slowly. "You know, Amy, I wouldn't blame you if you—if you wanted to hurt Jeanine. I know she's evil, and if she told people what she knows about you, you'd be in very serious danger. So . . . so I understand why you might want to . . . to . . ."

Amy finished the sentence for her. "Why I might want to kill Jeanine?"

Tasha didn't speak or nod. But in Amy's mind, she didn't need to do either.

"You *do*," she said in a hushed voice. "You believe what they're saying."

"Don't be silly," Tasha murmured, but her voice was unconvincing.

With one last look of utter despair, Amy turned her back on her best friend and ran the rest of the way to school.

But school provided no haven for Amy. Even as she was climbing the steps to the main door, she knew something was going on. And it was all about her.

She could actually feel eyes on her as she walked to her locker. People she spoke to barely replied. They seemed to be stepping out of her way, avoiding her like the plague. Even her homeroom teacher looked at her oddly. And she was absolutely certain that the desks on either side had been moved farther from hers.

Throughout the day, she caught snippets of whispered conversations in the halls and in her classrooms.

"She's always hated Jeanine, since first grade. They used to fight all the time."

"She must have thought just falling down the stairs would kill her."

"I wonder what she hit her with?"

"It must have been a real shock when she found out Jeanine was still alive."

"That's why she went to the hospital and pulled out her feeding tube."

Not true, Amy wanted to scream. Not true, not true, none of it is true! But she said nothing to anyone. Not that anyone seemed interested in hearing anything she had to say. She found herself walking alone, her head down, scurrying from one class to the next. At lunchtime she hid in an empty classroom.

While she was in there, Mr. Nevins came in to empty the wastebasket. The custodian stared at her for a second, and he scowled before leaving. Surely he'd heard the rumors about her too.

She considered going to the clinic, pretending to be

sick and asking the nurse to call her mother. Or just leaving school. But it would seem like she was running away. And she'd only look guiltier.

So, somehow, she made it through the day, her face red from the burning shame of knowing everyone was talking about her. The very instant the last bell rang, she was out the front door and on her way home.

She'd only been walking for a minute when she heard Eric yelling to her. "Amy, wait!"

She stopped and allowed him to catch up. His face was flushed and his eyes were wide. He was clearly distressed.

"Do you know what people are saying about you?" he asked.

She was grateful to hear that at least he sounded incredulous. "Do you believe them, Eric?" she asked.

"Of course not!"

Tasha caught up with them, panting. "Amy, we have to talk!"

"Eric was telling me people are gossiping about me."

Eric shook his head in wonderment. "It's really stupid. But I guess everyone knows you and Jeanine are famous rivals."

Tasha agreed with him. "And Eric and I know there's an even bigger reason for you to want Jeanine's mouth permanently shut."

All the awfulness of the day rose to the surface, and Amy turned to Tasha in a fury. "And what's my reason, Tasha? What's my problem with Jeanine? That Jeanine found out the truth about me? That *someone* told Jeanine the truth about me. And I'm starting to think that maybe I know who that someone is!"

Tasha caught her meaning immediately. "Amy! You know I didn't tell her!"

"That's what you say!" Amy shot back.

Tasha was outraged. "I can't believe you just said that!"

Amy was just as furious. "I can't believe you said what you said!"

"Hey, you guys, cut it out," Eric protested.

Amy was more than willing to cut the conversation short. Just as she had run to school that morning, she ran all the way home.

Her mother wasn't back from the university yet. Amy roamed the house, upstairs and downstairs, as if movement would stir up something in her head, an idea, a plan, a way to get out of this horrible mess. She was caught up in a real nightmare, the wide-awake kind.

She couldn't stand it. She had to talk to her mother, Dr. Hopkins . . . an adult, someone who still believed in her and could tell her what to do.

She went to the phone. The blinking light on the answering machine told her there were messages. She hit Play.

"Amy Candler should be arrested and tortured and made to spend the rest of her life in jail!" *Beep*.

Amy thought she recognized Linda Riviera's voice. But the next voice was totally unfamiliar.

"This is a message for Amy Candler. My name is Fran Carpenter, I'm a reporter from the *National Star*, and I'm writing an article on preteen killers. Your name was passed on to me today, and I'd like very much to interview you."

Amy's stomach churned as the reporter recited her phone number. At least the next message was normal.

"Hi, honey, it's Mom. My class was canceled, and David and I are going to the farmers' market. We should be home around five."

Amy didn't hear the usual beep. Instead, there were a scratching sound and a clunk, as if the phone had been set down on something hard.

Then she heard a voice, a bit hollow, as if it was coming from a distance. "Would you like to stay for dinner tonight, David?"

"Sure, but I'm going to do the cooking."

"You can cook?"

"It's a surprise for you. I've been taking cooking

lessons. Tonight you and Amy will be enjoying a gourmet dinner. Unless, of course, I mess up and we end up ordering pizza."

There was a laugh, and then a high-pitched screeching sound. "What was that?" Amy heard her mother ask.

"It was the phone. You have to press a button to hang up. Let me have it."

There was another scratchy sound. Finally the machine issued its beep and went silent.

Amy was silent too. Because now she knew how Jeanine had learned that Amy was a clone.

It was the mobile phone, Dr. Hopkins's mobile phone. Amy had called Jeanine on it the past week and left a message on Jeanine's answering machine. But she wasn't accustomed to mobile phones and hadn't turned it off properly. And Jeanine had heard Amy and Tasha and Dr. Hopkins talking about the fact that she was a clone.

An enormous rush of guilt flooded Amy. She remembered what she'd said to Tasha that day, and she felt terrible. How could she ever have suspected that Tasha would betray her?

But on the other hand, was it any worse than Tasha's believing that Amy had tried to kill Jeanine? Amy clutched her head and tried to subdue a feeling of panic. What was happening to her world?

The phone rang. Amy stared at it for a second and then snatched it up. "Hello?"

The voice on the other end was muffled, as if someone was speaking through a tissue. "Amy Candler, you're going to end up in the electric chair."

In the background she could hear another voice. "There's no more electric chair, dummy! They use lethal injections now." Then the phone went dead.

Amy replaced the receiver. She supposed she had better get used to receiving this kind of prank call. It would go on.

Jeanine had been struck on the head and pushed down a flight of stairs.

In the hospital her feeding tube had been pulled out.

Someone was definitely trying to kill her.

And the chief suspect was Amy.

Yes, these calls would go on.

Until Amy figured out who was really trying to kill Jeanine Bryant.

eleven

Amy ran upstairs to her bedroom. Sitting down at her desk, she opened a spiral notebook to a clean page. At the top of the page, in all capital letters, she wrote PEOPLE WHO HATE JEANINE BRYANT.

There were the blackmail victims, of course. Under the heading she wrote *Simone Cusack,* and under that *Dirt Sanders.* Tasha had told her once about a very clumsy girl in phys ed whom Jeanine teased mercilessly. Amy didn't know her name, so she just wrote *Clumsy PE Girl.* Back in September, Jeanine had reported a boy in her math class for cheating on a test. It turned out that she was just getting back at him for stepping on her foot and he hadn't cheated at all. Amy added *Alan Greenfield* to the list.

There were more. At Simone's party, Layne certainly hadn't appreciated Jeanine's remark about her sister's eating disorder. Maybe Layne was even angrier than she'd seemed. *Layne Hunter.* And there was the boy Jeanine had flirted with like crazy when all she wanted from him was help with setting up a computer. As soon as the computer was running, she'd dropped him. *Bobby Marcus.*

Then Amy thought back over all the years she'd known Jeanine and all the crummy things Jeanine had done to people.

Like the past year in gymnastics. Doing a series of cartwheels, Jeanine had collided with another gymnast, one of the best in the class, Amber Gillette. It looked like Jeanine had done it on purpose. In any case, Amber had twisted her ankle badly and had been out for weeks. Later Amy heard that the injury had caused permanent damage to a ligament and Amber could forget about ever getting into a real gymnastics competition. Yes, Amber had a good reason to hate Jeanine, and Amy added her name to the list.

And that time in the fifth grade when Jeanine didn't land the big part in the Christmas play but only got to be the understudy. The girl who did get the part came down with the flu just before the performance, so Jeanine took over. Kids said that Jeanine had somehow managed to give the girl the flu on purpose. That would be hard to prove, though. . . .

But Amy had a clear memory of a birthday party long ago when Jeanine had removed the head of someone's Malibu Barbie and announced that Barbie was now dead. Barbie's owner had been beside herself.

Amy put her pen down. The list was getting longer and longer, but people didn't try to kill each other over a headless Barbie.

She ripped the page out of the notebook, crumpled it, and tossed it in the wastebasket. Then she started on a fresh page.

PEOPLE WHO *REALLY REALLY REALLY* HATE JEANINE BRYANT.

The two blackmail victims. Three, if she counted herself. Which meant there had to be others. But how could she find out who they were?

Carrie seemed to be the kind of person who always knew what was going on at school. After checking in the school directory for Carrie's number, Amy picked up the phone and punched it in.

A man answered. "Hello?"

"Hello, this is Amy Candler, can I speak to Carrie, please?"

"Just a minute," the man said pleasantly. "Carrie!" he

called. There was no response. "Hang on," the man told Amy. He put the phone down, and he must have moved away because his voice became fainter. Amy could still hear him, though. "Carrie!"

Then she heard Carrie's voice. "What, Dad?"

"There's a phone call for you. Amy Candler."

There was a silence. Amy strained to hear.

"I don't want to talk to her," Carrie said.

"Well, I'm not going to tell her that," her father said.

"Tell her I'm in the shower!"

The man returned to the phone. "I'm sorry, Amy, she's in the shower. I'll tell her to call you back."

"Thank you," Amy said glumly. She hung up the phone, knowing perfectly well not to expect a return phone call from Carrie. After a moment she tried calling Layne.

Layne was in the shower too. Hanging up the phone, Amy shivered. Suddenly she felt very, very cold.

She heard the front door open downstairs and ran out of her room. "Mom?" she called.

"Hi, honey!"

She ran down the stairs. Her mom wasn't alone. Both she and Dr. Hopkins had their arms filled with grocery bags, and they were both laughing about something. Dr. Hopkins greeted her warmly.

"Hi, Amy. Listen, get on the phone, call all your

friends, and tell them to come over for dinner. We bought way too much food!"

"I don't have any friends," Amy murmured, but no one heard her. She felt torn. On the one hand, she wanted to tell her mother what was going on. On the other hand, her mother looked like she was having such a nice day, Amy didn't want to spoil it.

So she went through the motions of helping with dinner, set the table with the good china, and even managed to eat. Fortunately, her mother and Dr. Hopkins were having such a good time, talking and laughing, that neither seemed to notice that Amy wasn't saying much at all.

After dinner, she claimed to have a ton of homework and went back to her room. There she looked at her revised suspect list again. *Simone Cusack, Dirt Sanders.* Amy had read enough mystery novels and she'd seen enough detective shows on TV to know that a true suspect had to have motive, means, and opportunity. The motive was the same for both—they were being blackmailed. As for means—well, it wasn't like Jeanine had been shot. Anyone could push another person down the stairs or pull a tube out of an arm.

And they both had opportunity—school and jobs at Northside Hospital. Amy stared at the two names, as if one of them might suddenly pop off the page and announce "I'm guilty." When the phone rang, she jumped.

But she didn't answer it. She just couldn't deal with another nasty anonymous caller. She let her mother pick up the phone downstairs, and she waited.

"Amy!"

She went out into the hallway. "Yes?"

"It's Eric on the phone."

Amy bit her lip. She really didn't want to talk to anyone.

"I'll call him back," she yelled. "Tell him—tell him I'm in the shower."

And then, so she wouldn't feel like a rotten liar, she did take a shower. But she didn't call Eric back.

The next morning she pretended to have a special student council meeting at school. That gave her an excuse to grab a granola bar instead of sitting down to breakfast, and to leave the house before anyone came by for her. She was hoping to be the first person to arrive at school so she could hang around the entrance and watch for Dirt Sanders. She had some questions for him. As for Simone Cusack, Amy planned to corner her after school. With the right questions, she might be able to trip one of them up and one of them might confess.

If not, maybe she'd be able to read guilt in one of their faces. That wouldn't be the best evidence, though. She doubted it would stand up in court.

But she wasn't the first student to arrive at school. More than the usual number of extracurricular activities seemed to be scheduled that morning, and while the school wasn't packed yet, there were plenty of kids. As Amy hung around the entrance, she detected a distinct chill in the air. And it had nothing to do with the weather.

Clearly the word had spread and had saturated the school population. People she knew barely glanced in her direction. People she didn't know looked at her with expressions that ranged from curious to horrified. It was like they could all see the cloud of suspicion that hung over her head. She didn't know how she was going to make it through the day.

And she could no longer bear standing by the school entrance for everyone to see and gawk at as they came into the building. So she hurried off to sit alone in homeroom.

But before she even opened the classroom door, she spotted someone through the window. It was Linda Riviera.

Linda wasn't on Amy's list of suspects—in fact, she

was the last person in the world Amy would ever suspect of hurting Jeanine. But Linda might have some very valuable information. If she was really and truly a best friend to Jeanine, the two of them had no secrets from each other. Linda had to know about Jeanine's blackmail scheme. And she'd probably know the names of all the people involved.

Amy opened the door softly. "Linda?"

The girl turned to face her. What little color there was in Linda's pasty face instantly drained away. She jumped out of her seat. "Don't come any closer, Amy Candler, or I'll scream!"

Amy groaned. "Oh, come on, Linda, knock it off. I didn't push Jeanine down the stairs, I didn't take the feeding tube out of her arm, and I'm not trying to kill her. But if someone is really trying to kill Jeanine, I want to find out who that someone is."

Linda was backing away from her, holding her hands protectively in front of her face. Amy sighed in exasperation. "Linda, just *listen,* okay? I know that Jeanine's been blackmailing people. I know all about Simone and the bald guy, Dirt. And I know there have to be more people. And I'll bet you know who all those people are."

Linda didn't admit this, but she didn't deny it either.

And she'd stopped moving backward, which was a good sign.

"Don't you see, Linda? Those people have a reason for wanting Jeanine dead. They don't want to be paying a blackmailer forever. So it's got to be one of them!"

Linda raised a trembling arm and pointed. *"You're* one of them."

Amy tried desperately to ignore the wave of nausea that almost overcame her. So Linda knew about her too.

"Tell me who the others are," Amy demanded. When Linda didn't reply, Amy took a step toward her. Linda backed up to a wall and pressed herself against it. Amy almost wanted to laugh, but instead she made a sour face. If threatening Linda was the only way to get information out of her, so be it. "Tell me!"

Linda spoke in a high-pitched squeak. "Kristy Morris."

Amy was surprised. Kristy was in her biology class. She was a quiet, mousy girl who never said much. Amy couldn't imagine what kind of terrible secret Kristy was carrying.

"What was she blackmailing Kristy for?" she asked Linda.

"I don't know," Linda said. Amy took another step toward her, and Linda shrieked.

"Really, I don't know! Jeanine would never tell me what she was blackmailing people over. She said I was terrible at keeping secrets!"

Amy thought about that. It made sense. Linda was notorious for having a big mouth, and Jeanine was too smart to trust her valuable information with someone who might spread it around. Even if that person was her best friend.

But this was actually good news. At least it meant Linda didn't know that Amy was a clone. And Amy didn't really need to know *why* Jeanine was blackmailing other people—she just needed to know their names.

Behind her the classroom door opened and a hall monitor stuck her head in. She looked at the two girls suspiciously. "I heard someone yelling in here," she said. "What's going on?"

Linda ran toward the door. "She's after me!" she screamed. "Amy Candler's going to kill me!" She ran past the monitor and out into the hall.

The hall monitor must have been the only person at Parkside who didn't know the name Amy Candler. She just looked at Amy, shrugged, and closed the door.

Linda must have been really shook up, because she never came back to homeroom that morning. Amy wondered if she was having a nervous breakdown in the school clinic. Some kids drifted in, and then with the sound of the bell came the big rush of students. Ms. Weller called the roll, and the intercom crackled on.

"Please give your attention to the morning announcements. Jeanine Bryant remains in critical condition at Northside Hospital. Tickets for the girls' chorus performance are on sale in the Student Activities Office. Eighth-graders who are planning to go on the class trip must bring in their signed permissions by Friday. The diving club will meet at the swimming pool at three-fifteen this afternoon. Will Amy Candler please come to the office immediately?"

Not again, Amy thought miserably. She was sure Linda had complained about her. Reluctantly she got up and accepted a pass from Ms. Weller.

The halls were silent as she walked to the office, but as she approached the administration wing her ears picked up on a voice. It was coming from behind a door labeled CUSTODIAL SERVICES. Suddenly the door opened and Dirt Sanders came out. He looked even more sullen than usual. Just behind him was the custodian, Mr. Nevins.

"You better watch it, kid," Mr. Nevins was saying.

Dirt didn't acknowledge the warning. He just kept walking, his face fixed in a sour expression. Mr. Nevins went back into his office and closed the door.

Amy was sorely tempted to knock on the door. Did Mr. Nevins know something? Maybe he'd seen something at the hospital. Maybe he suspected Dirt too—and maybe he had some evidence!

"Amy!"

She turned. Dr. Noble was standing at the entrance to the main office. "We're waiting for you, Amy," she said.

"Yes, I'm coming," Amy said. She'd stop and see Mr. Nevins after speaking with Dr. Noble.

She wasn't surprised when she saw Linda Riviera in the principal's office. What did surprise her was the group of other people in attendance. There was the new school psychologist, Dr. Holland. A woman wearing a police uniform. And Amy's mother.

"Mom! What are you doing here?"

Her mother was pale. "I was called just twenty minutes ago and told to come here right away. Amy, what's going on?"

"There's been an official complaint made against your daughter," Dr. Noble said.

Amy looked at Linda and rolled her eyes. Linda shrank back into her seat. "It's not my fault!" she squealed.

Dr. Noble continued. "Linda's complaint came after the more serious accusation lodged by Mrs. Bryant at the police station. Mrs. Bryant believes that Amy is a danger to her daughter, Jeanine. This police officer has been sent here to question Amy, Ms. Candler."

The psychologist spoke up. "And I'm here to evaluate Amy. In fact, when we're finished here, I'd like to give Amy some standard personality tests."

Now it was the police officer's turn. "Amy, what were your intentions when you went into Jeanine's hospital room Monday afternoon?"

Nancy Candler stood up. "Excuse me, Officer. Are you here to arrest my daughter?"

"No, ma'am, I just have some questions."

"Then I would like to call my lawyer. I want him to be present during any questioning."

Amy felt like she'd suddenly walked onto the set of a police drama.

"Yes, ma'am," the policewoman said.

"Ms. Candler," Dr. Noble said, "I suggest that you take Amy home."

"Are you expelling her?" Nancy asked.

Dr. Noble shook her head. "Not without more concrete evidence. But our students can be a bit more impetuous in passing judgment. I think Amy would be safer at home today."

Nancy rose. "We're leaving now."

"But what about my tests?" the psychologist whined.

Nancy gave her a withering look that clearly stated what she thought of Dr. Holland's standard personality tests. She took Amy's hand as if Amy was a little kid, and for once Amy didn't mind. They left the office and the building.

twelve 12

By the time they arrived home, Nancy had heard the whole story. "Oh, honey, why didn't you tell me people suspected you?"

"I didn't want to worry you," Amy told her. "You've been looking so happy lately, with Dr. Hopkins."

Nancy bit her lip. "Oh, dear. Amy, there's nothing serious happening between David and me. We're just good friends."

Amy brushed that aside. "What are we going to do, Mom? What if they arrest me?"

"I'm calling the lawyer right now," Nancy said. She

left Amy in the living room and went into the kitchen to make the call. Amy flung herself on the sofa.

Was it really possible that she could be arrested for the attempted murder of Jeanine Bryant? On TV, and in real life, people were wrongly accused all the time.

Her mother returned. "The lawyer wasn't there, but I left a message on his machine. I'm sure he'll get back to us right away."

The mention of the answering machine reminded Amy of something else she wanted to tell her mother. "I figured out how Jeanine found out about me," she said, and she related her experience of the day before, when she had heard her mother and Dr. Hopkins talking after they'd thought the cellular phone was disconnected.

Her mother looked a little nervous. "Exactly what did you hear David and me saying to each other?"

Amy rolled her eyes. "Hey, I've got bigger problems right now than worrying about my mother's love life."

There was a flicker of smile on her mother's face. "Everything's going to be okay, honey. We'll deal with this." She put an arm around Amy. "Would you like something to eat? Are you hungry?"

Amy was surprised to realize that she actually was hungry. Even though she was still in big trouble, knowing that her mother was on her side made her feel a zillion times better. "Starving," she replied.

So at a time when some people were just sitting down to breakfast, Amy and her mother heated up the leftovers of the fancy beef dish that Dr. Hopkins had made. It was weird to be eating at nine-thirty in the morning, but the day had started off weird and it looked like it was going to stay that way. After stuffing themselves on beef and broccoli with cheese sauce, they curled up together on the sofa and watched talk shows and soap operas. For once Amy felt like her own problems were as big as anything she saw or heard about on these programs.

By the time the sun set, Amy was starting to feel hungry again. Her mother, however, was fidgeting for a different reason. "I can't believe the lawyer hasn't called back yet," she grumbled. "I just can't sit here and do nothing while my daughter's been wrongly accused of a crime." She hopped off the sofa. "Let's go."

"Go where?" Amy asked.

"To Northside Hospital. I'm sure Mrs. Bryant will be there. I want to talk to her."

Amy forgot her hunger. She wanted to go too—not to talk to Mrs. Bryant, but to keep an eye on Jeanine's room, and to make sure Dirt Sanders didn't go in there.

But she found out right away that she wasn't going

to get anywhere near Jeanine. When Amy and her mother got off the elevator on the fifth floor, they saw Mrs. Bryant talking with a young doctor by the nurses' station. Mrs. Bryant saw them too. Her face turned red, and she looked ready to explode.

Nancy hurried over to her and placed a gentle hand on the woman's arm. "I must talk to you," she said softly. "Please."

Mrs. Bryant stiffened, but at least she didn't scream. The doctor seemed relieved at having an excuse to escape. "I'll stop by and see Jeanine later," he told Mrs. Bryant before going into an office behind the nurses' station. Amy could see him through the large window as he sat down at a little table with a nurse.

Mrs. Bryant glared at Amy. "I don't want you going near my daughter." She turned to the two nurses who were behind the station's desk. "Did you hear me? This child is not to be allowed in Jeanine's room."

The nurses nodded, and Mrs. Bryant turned back to Amy's mother. "What do you want to tell me?"

"Let's sit down over there," Nancy urged, indicating a small waiting area with sofas and chairs. Amy started to follow them, but Nancy shook her head. "Amy, please wait by the nurses' station."

So Amy hung around the nurses, wishing she could at least see Jeanine's room from there. She knew it was just a short distance away, but with nothing else to do, she looked through the window behind the nurses' station. The young doctor and the nurse were still sitting at the table, talking. The glass must have been truly soundproof, because she couldn't hear anything they were saying. But feeling bored, she decided to read their lips.

"Do you think the Bryant girl can survive?" the nurse was asking the doctor.

"Possibly," he said. "But she's had severe brain damage. If she does come out of this coma, I doubt that she'll have any mental or physical capabilities left."

Amy shuddered. Jeanine's situation was worse than she'd thought. Sure, Jeanine was rotten to the core, and the fact that she was lying comatose in a hospital bed didn't make her a better person, but she was still a human being. Amy was truly sad.

A noise coming from the end of the corridor distracted her. Simone was headed her way, pushing a small cart covered with magazines. The sight of the magazines made something click in Amy's head.

She walked over to Simone. When Simone saw her, her face became stricken. She stood very still. "What do you want?" she asked.

"The last time I saw you, you were pushing this cart out of Jeanine's room," Amy said.

"Yeah, so?"

"Jeanine's in a coma!" Amy said. "She can't read. Why did you bring her magazines?"

Jeanine's doctor passed them, and while he was within hearing distance, Simone just looked at her defiantly. After the doctor had turned the corner, she replied, "It's the rule. We're supposed to stop in every room, no matter what's wrong with the patient. Excuse me, I have to get to work."

But Amy put a restraining hand on the cart. "There's something else I want to ask you. How did you get the bracelet back?"

Simone's eyes filled with fear. Or was it guilt? Amy couldn't read the expression. But either way, Amy had a sudden feeling that she should check on Jeanine. She stepped aside and let Simone pass. Then she glanced over at the nurses' station.

The nurses must have been with patients, because only the clerk was there now. Quickly, silently, Amy made her way down the hall and around the corner.

She could see Jeanine's room, and she made a bee-line for it. She'd almost reached the door when she heard a noise from the stairway behind her. Someone was coming.

She had to make a split-second decision—run back to the nurses' station, where she was supposed to be waiting, or go into Jeanine's room and run the risk of getting caught.

But she didn't have a chance to decide.

Suddenly Jeanine's door burst open and a huge cart piled with towels and sheets came bursting out. It was a repeat of her experience coming off the elevator—only this time the cart didn't waver from side to side. It was heading directly toward Amy, and there was no time to get out of the way.

Amy threw up her hands—not defensively, but straight out in front of her. With effort, she was able to stop the cart, and she darted around it to see who was pushing it.

She caught only a glimpse of the person before he ran into the stairwell, practically colliding with the doctor who was coming out. But a glimpse was all Amy needed. The shiny bald head was a dead giveaway. Before she took off in pursuit, she took a quick look at the girl lying in the hospital bed inside the room. The girl whose face was now covered by a big white pillow.

Amy tore into the room and bent over Jeanine. "Step back!" ordered a voice from the door. Jeanine's doctor ran in and pulled the pillow off Jeanine's face. Then he put his stethoscope on her chest.

He ran past Amy and into the hall. "Code Blue!" he yelled. "Room five oh five! Code Blue!"

Nurses came running down the hall. Mrs. Bryant was running after them. "That girl! She's trying to kill my daughter!"

Amy couldn't waste any time hanging around to defend herself. Dirt Sanders had gotten a good head start.

But Dirt Sanders wasn't a genetically engineered clone. At top speed, Amy rushed to the stairwell and took the stairs five at a time. There was no sign of Dirt, but Amy concentrated on her listening skills and followed the distant sound of running footsteps. And as the pounding grew louder, she knew she was getting closer. She heard a stairway door below her swing shut.

With only two quick leaps, she made it to the bottom of the stairs and flew out the door. Now she could actually see the bald head in front of her. And it took only one flying leap for her to tackle him.

"I've got you!" she yelled triumphantly.

"Get off me!" Dirt yelled back. "You've got the wrong person!"

But Amy had watched a lot of television. And she knew the bad guys always said that.

thirteen

Lying on Dirt's back, she grabbed his arms and pulled them around so she could hold them as if her own hands were handcuffs. Then she realized she was in a basement and there didn't seem to be anyone around. She'd never tried to see if her voice could be louder than other voices, but now was the time to find out.

"I've got him!" she bellowed, hoping her voice would carry up at least one flight. "I've got him!"

"I'm not him!" Dirt yelled. "Get off me!"

Amy experienced a moment of doubt. After all,

she'd only seen him from the back, and lots of guys were bald. "Turn around," she ordered him.

"I can't if you don't get off my back!"

Still holding his wrists tightly, Amy moved enough so he could turn his head. She hadn't made any mistake. The person she'd seen was definitely Dirt.

"He's hiding in the supply closet!" Dirt declared. "Over there, on the right!"

"Who's hiding in the supply closet?" Amy demanded.

"The man who smothered Jeanine!"

Amy hesitated. What was Dirt up to? Was he just trying to confuse her so that she'd release him and he could take off?

But now that she was looking directly into his eyes, she had an instinctive feeling that he was telling the truth. She tore her eyes from his face to look at the door labeled SUPPLY CLOSET and listened closely.

Someone *was* in the closet. And whoever it was must have heard them, because suddenly a man burst out and ran toward an exit.

Amy again relied on her instinct to make a decision. She released Dirt and flew toward the running figure. She leaped onto his back, but this person was bigger than Dirt, and he tried to push her off. Then she saw his face.

"Mr. Nevins!"

Now Dirt was by her side. And between the two of them they pulled the custodian to the floor.

"He was always lurking around Jeanine's room," Dirt told her, panting furiously. "I think he's the one who put her here in the first place!"

"Is that true?" Amy yelled at the struggling man. "Did you try to kill Jeanine?"

"None of your business!" Mr. Nevins shouted.

"I'm making it my business," Amy shouted back. "Did you try to kill Jeanine Bryant?"

Mr. Nevins uttered an obscene word, which made her even angrier. She grabbed one of his legs and pulled it back. The custodian screamed in pain.

"Answer me!" Amy yelled. Mr. Nevins let out another shriek. Amy gave the leg a second hard tug. "Answer me!"

"Okay, okay! I had to get rid of her! She was blackmailing me!"

And suddenly Amy knew why. "You're the one who's been stealing all the supplies and equipment at school! Jeanine found out about it! You hit her on the head and pushed her down the stairs, right?" When she didn't get an answer, she gave the custodian's leg another jerk.

"Arghhh!" he screamed. "You're going to rip my leg off!"

"Did you push Jeanine down the stairs?"

"Yes! Yes! I pushed her down the stairs!"

"And you ripped out her feeding tube?"

"Yes!"

"And you just smothered her with a pillow?"

"Yes! I shut her up for good. Now let go, you're killing me!"

"I heard that!" came a voice from the stairwell, and a security guard appeared with his gun drawn. Just behind him was Jeanine's doctor. The guard was pointing the gun at the custodian and yelling "Don't move!" The doctor, however, was staring at Amy and her grip on Mr. Nevins's leg. Quickly she let go and stood up. Dirt rose too.

"Get these kids away from me!" Mr. Nevins shrieked. "I'm innocent!"

"Forget it, fella," the guard barked. "I heard your confession."

"I didn't mean it. I was just saying that to get her off me! She forced me to say it! She was about to rip my leg off!"

"Yeah, right," the guard said. He glanced at Amy. "You're what, young lady, about five feet tall? A hundred pounds? Sorry, fella, your confession stands. Little girls like this can't rip legs off big guys like you. Now get up!"

Mr. Nevins tried to move, then let out another yelp of pain. "I can't! My leg's broken!"

The doctor was still looking in disbelief at Amy. "He must have fallen on his leg," she said quickly. Then she smiled sweetly and tried to look as young and innocent as she could. Fortunately, the doctor was distracted by the arrival of police officers, who took charge of the situation. One of them was the same officer who had appeared at school that morning to question Amy. Her mouth dropped open when she saw Amy standing at the scene.

"You again! You can't stay out of trouble, can you?"

"It's just a coincidence," Amy said weakly.

While the police took charge of getting Mr. Nevins on a stretcher so he could be hauled away, Amy and Dirt followed the doctor back up the five flights of stairs. Just outside Jeanine's room, Mrs. Bryant was sobbing on the shoulder of a nurse. When she saw Amy, she cried out, "There she is, that's the murderer! She smothered my daughter!"

The nurse supporting her spoke soothingly. "No, Mrs. Bryant, that's not possible. A child her size wouldn't have the strength to do something like that." She led Jeanine's weeping mother away.

Now Amy could see her own mother standing in the hall. She rushed over, and Nancy wrapped her arms around her. "Is Jeanine dead?" Amy asked in a whisper.

"Yes, honey," her mother said. She stroked Amy's hair.

Amy was suddenly overcome by tears. There was no denying the fact that she had despised Jeanine. Jeanine had been a formidable enemy for a long time.

In a strange way, Amy knew she would miss her.

fourteen
14

"So Dirt Sanders isn't such a bad guy after all," Eric mused.

"Nah," Amy replied. "He just wants to look like one."

"I still don't understand how Simone got the bracelet back," Tasha said.

"Easy," Amy told her. "She went through Jeanine's bag at the hospital and took it."

"Really? She went through Jeanine's bag while Jeanine was in a coma?" Tasha frowned. "That doesn't sound like Simone. It's not a very nice thing to do."

"It's not stealing if you're taking back something that belongs to you," Amy said.

They were on their way to school the next morning, and Amy was filling them in on the details. But she wasn't enjoying herself much as she told the tale. "I still can't believe you guys suspected me," she said.

"*I* didn't suspect you!" Eric declared indignantly. "It was my stupid sister here who had suspicions."

Amy gave him a stern look. "Yeah, well, you didn't knock yourself out defending me."

Eric hung his head. "Sorry about that," he said. He looked so cute and humble, Amy automatically forgave him.

It wasn't as easy with Tasha, though. "Did you really think I could kill someone?" Amy asked her.

Tasha didn't answer. Instead, she asked her own question. "Did *you* really think I'd tell anyone your secret?"

Amy couldn't respond. Neither of them had trusted the other. What kind of best friends were they, anyway?

"We still don't know how many other people Jeanine was blackmailing," Tasha remarked.

"And I don't think we ever will," Amy said.

"I guess it doesn't matter anyway," Tasha said. "I mean, Jeanine's dead."

Amy shivered. "Poor Jeanine."

Eric looked at her in surprise. "You really feel bad about her, don't you?"

Amy nodded. "I keep thinking back to the first fight we ever had. It was in the first grade, and we both wanted to be the leader when our class lined up to walk to lunch. The teacher picked me."

Eric was startled. "That's why she became your enemy? Because you were at the head of the line?"

Amy nodded. "It was a pretty big deal in first grade. And she could never forgive and forget. Poor Jeanine." Again she shivered.

"Are you cold?" Eric asked her.

"No, I was just thinking . . . I've never known anyone my age who died before."

"Me neither," Tasha said. "It makes you realize how much you should appreciate life."

"Yeah," Amy said.

"And—and friends," Tasha added. "Especially best friends."

"Best friends are very important," Amy agreed. "Too bad Jeanine couldn't be anyone's best friend, not even Linda Riviera's, really."

Eric was looking at them both with concern in his eyes. "So you two are still best friends, right?"

"Sure," Tasha said quickly.

"Of course," Amy echoed. This was pretty much

151

true. She might not be feeling like a best friend to Tasha at this very moment, but she figured she'd get over it. Forgive and forget, that was what she had to do.

She was a little nervous as they approached Parkside. Had the news of what happened at the hospital made it through the school yet? Would everyone know that Mr. Nevins, not Amy, was the villain? She didn't think she could take one more day of icy stares and whispered accusations from her classmates.

But the word seemed to have spread fast. Before she even reached her locker, a dozen people had called out greetings to her, and even more had given her big warm smiles. Some people made it very clear that they considered her a hero. There was definitely a thaw in the air.

Amy couldn't say everything was back to normal. The events of the past week and a half meant that nothing would ever be normal again.

But then, when had things ever been normal for her before?

Don't miss

replica

#11
Lucky Thirteen

Amy thinks being perfect can be a real drag. Everyone expects her to behave responsibly and to use her extraordinary talents for good. But when she meets one of her clones—an unexpected Amy, Number Thirteen, who goes by the name of Aly—she gets a taste of "normal" teen life and wants more.

Aly is a reject from Project Crescent.

She runs with a wild crowd whose motto is Good Times Now!

She convinces Amy to hang loose and have fun.

Drawn to Aly's sense of freedom, Amy rejects her genetic roots. But Aly's carefree ways come at a high cost. . . .